Also by J. Mercer:

Triplicity
After They Go
Dark & Stormy

Perfection and Other Illusive Things

by J. Mercer

Published 2020 / Bare Ink
Printed in the United States of America
Print ISBN: 978-1-7321332-9-7
E-ISBN: 978-1-7348883-0-0
Library of Congress Control Number:
Perfection and Other Illusive Things / written by J Mercer

Cover design © Robin Vuchnich
Edited by Staci Frenes

This book is a work of fiction. Names, characters, places, and incidents are either
the product of the author's imagination or are used fictitiously. Any resemblance
to actual events, companies, or persons, living or dead, is entirely coincidental.

Designations used by manufacturers and sellers to distinguish their products are
claimed trademarks. Where those designations appear in this book, and the
publisher and author are aware, the designations have been capitalized.

For all the types of girls,
that you see yourselves truly and remember what's
important. Illusions will never be the path to happiness.

Table of Contents

"Don't believe everything you think."

– Allan Lokos

Tuesday

I hid the school newspaper from my best friend.

Billie wouldn't appreciate that I wasn't reading the *news* part of it, and she'd roll her eyes when she realized it was Hawk's words I was melting over. *Him again?* she'd say. *Honestly, Eden. He's going to be working at a gas station for the rest of his life.*

Except we didn't even know if he worked at a gas station in the first place. Her point, of course, was that I wasn't the type of girl to date a guy who'd end up in a job like that. My point, if I actually felt like having the conversation, was that his words were perfection and clearly he was more of an intellect than she took him for.

Mr. Keller clapped and I startled, crumpling the paper in my hands. I resisted the urge to smooth it on my thigh and draw attention to the fact that I wasn't listening in class, because, you guessed it, I also wasn't the type of girl to not listen in class.

"Your semester project will, of course, end with a thoughtful essay—psychology applied, if you will—but for starters I just want you to pick something, preferably something you don't like very much, and make a list of pros and cons for it. I'm going to give you some time to work on this, and then we'll get into the details later—what the next step will be. Sound good? As it's a large part of your grade, make sure you put a little thought into it."

Something I didn't like very much? But everything I wasn't supposed to like, I did like: Hawk's poems, Hawk himself, the watch my grandpa gave me right before he died...it had been my grandma's and this morning, in the drizzle that he loved, I'd almost put it on. Then I heard Billie's words in my ear: "Watches are obsolete." And my mom's: "That old thing? Does it even work?"

It did, actually. Well, sometimes. When it wanted to. But even if it didn't, I'd still love it. It was gold and vintage and delicate.

When I put it on, though, I was reminded of how *not* delicate I was. Not that strong, independent girls like me were supposed to want to be delicate. Strong and sturdy made for good volleyball players, and I was supposed to care about what my body could do, not what it looked like.

And no, I didn't want to be delicate only because Hawk's best friend Ivy was ethereal. Or because the girls he went for were usually as thin as her. A girl like me didn't have a chance with a guy like him anyway. Or, as Billie would put it, a guy like him didn't have a chance with a girl like me.

Frankly, I was pretty sick of being a girl like me.

Girls like me did what they were supposed to, that's what I'd come to realize. Not what they wanted. Girls like Ivy did what they wanted, and, it seemed to me, seldom what they were supposed to. There had to be a happy medium. There had to be an in-between.

The bell rang and I stuffed the crumpled paper into my pocket.

"What are you doing your list on?" Billie asked, collecting her stuff from the desk next to mine.

"My grandma's watch." It was the only thing in my head. It just came out.

"You're supposed to pick something you don't like. Were you even listening?"

"No one else likes it, though. Maybe my pros will convince them."

"Wes likes it."

I refrained from rolling my eyes. "Wes likes everything."

She winked. "Wes likes everything to do with you."

Yeah, yeah, I wanted to say. A girl like me would date a guy like Wes. Only, Billie and I had been best friends with him and Isaac for so long that when he'd kissed me three months ago, it felt more like kissing my grandpa. And when we managed to

3

still act like best friends the next day, it seemed better that way.

See, I had everything a girl like me should want: stellar grades, early admission to my third-choice college, a solid spot on the volleyball team, the most loyal best friend, the sweetest little brother, a mom who loved me, et cetera.

It wasn't that I didn't want those things; obviously, they were very nice things. It was just I wanted things outside that box too. Things Billie didn't understand. Things my mom wouldn't understand. Or Wes. Obviously, because he thought I should want him. So if I didn't want the things a girl like me should want, then maybe I wasn't really that girl anymore. And what was I supposed to do with that?

Maybe I should do my project—the pros and cons—on me.

Maybe I should do it on the girl I was supposed to be.

Wednesday

I stood in front of the bathroom mirror the next morning, trying to figure out what I was seeing.

It was me that I was looking at, except a better version. Like I was walking around with a permanent filter, one that didn't require me to take a selfie and apply.

There was a narrowing of my face, a widening of my eyes...

Taking a step to the bathroom counter, I leaned over to pull at my lips. They were fuller. And my nose, somehow overnight it had thinned out, becoming slighter than the one I'd had before.

Yesterday.

The one I'd had yesterday.

With a shake of my head, I rubbed my eyes, then reassessed one more time. I'd done this seven times now, and nothing had changed.

Well, nothing had changed since I'd woken up. Things had

definitely changed since last night: my eyelashes were longer, my hair darker and thicker. So much thicker. So much *better*.

My shoulders, I swear they used to be broader. My stomach, thighs and rear end, they used to be curvier.

As I stood there staring, a prickle crawled up my spine. Things like this didn't happen, not even in movies, unless you paid some terrible price. It couldn't be this easy.

My mom shouted that breakfast was ready, so I did my best to shake the tingle off and dropped my clothes where I was standing. I jumped into the water before realizing my grandma's watch, which I'd put on last night before bed, was still on my wrist.

I almost took it off, considering it wasn't waterproof, but it didn't work right anyway. And what if it held the magic of the new me in the mirror? Except there was no such thing as magic. I hadn't done any drugs in my seventeen years, so no hallucinations. Maybe I was losing my mind.

"Eden!" My mom poked her head into our little bathroom as I was rinsing my hair. "What's taking you so long? You're going to be late for school."

What was taking me so long? I laughed. I couldn't help it.

She frowned. I could see it through the water, the steam, and the frosted glass door. Her frowns were powerful, always had been.

Sticking my head out, I crossed my chest and stared at her. "Look at me."

"I'm looking."

"Look at my face."

"It's lovely, honey. Now get out."

She left and I turned the water off, grabbed my towel, and wiped the mirror clear of steam to catch another glimpse of the magic. That's what I'd call it for now.

Still the perfect lashes, thick with water and heavy like no amount of mascara could have made them yesterday. And my nose... I touched it, ran my fingers over it, felt for the little bump that was no longer there. I glanced at the watch, no longer looking so awkward on my thick wrist. Was I delicate now too?

"Eden!" Mom's tone snapped at me from down the hall, like a rubber band.

I slipped into my room, where there was no full-length mirror (because they only perpetuated society's misguided priorities of looks and materialism) and felt myself in bits as I got dressed. How many times had I cupped my palm over my belly, wishing it were flat? And now it was. Or that my butt—which had morphed my mom's childhood nickname for me ("Cheeks") into a derogatory term referring to its size—would no longer draw the same kind of attention. The thighs that forced me to buy a size up in jeans, so the waist was always a little too loose and I had to fight with them to stay up? Not so bulgy. I dug out a smaller pair and they were the perfect fit.

I made it to the kitchen like I'd arrived somewhere after a

long trip or had single-handedly won a volleyball game—not that I was that good, but a girl could dream. "Do I look different to you?"

My little brother blinked up at me and my mom sighed. "What?" she asked.

"Do I look *different* to you?"

She barely studied me before going back to her toast. "Did you cut your hair?"

"No, why, does it look fuller?" I beamed. *Yes, it does, Mom, it does look fuller.*

"I was just guessing." She gave me an exasperated sigh. "Eden, you seriously don't have time for this. Tell me what's different and let's get on with it."

"Just guess, please?"

She ran her gaze over me a little more thoroughly this time. "Your top's a little saggy. Are you trying to get money for new clothes?"

"Saggy? Mom, it's new!"

"It doesn't look new."

"It is!" My grin was hurting my cheeks. She might not be in tune to the magic like I was, maybe because she was too old to see it, but she obviously noticed something or she wouldn't have nailed the hair and waist right off the bat. "You see it, right, Reese?"

He shrugged. "You look nice."

"Are you saying you lost weight?" my mom asked. "You

don't need to lose weight. What you need is to eat breakfast."

Tapping grandma's watch, I pointed out, "I don't have time for breakfast."

"Skipping breakfast is not the way to lose weight."

"Take my orange," Reese said, handing it to me.

Linking pinkies with him like we did when we wanted to pull each other closer, I kissed his forehead and whispered, "I don't want your orange. And anyway, I'm late."

Girls like me were never late for school.

But maybe I wasn't that girl anymore. Maybe now I was the type of girl I wanted to be: more delicate and dainty on the outside, yet brighter, bolder, and a lot less worried about toeing the line. Regardless, I had to get to class. Grabbing my backpack, I ran out the front door, across the street, and onto the sidewalk that lined the football field. As I rushed past it, I picked up my pace—the school grounds were quiet, which implied how very late I was, but I did my best not to panic. I'd never been late to school, except once in eighth grade because of a dentist appointment. Hopefully, that would keep me out of trouble. I should've had Mom write a note.

But whatever, I looked freaking awesome, as the car window I passed was telling me. And the next one. And a truck's large side-view mirror. All of them in perfect agreement, and each time I smiled with relief and surprise. Truth was, if I had to trade a perfect me for one tardy, I'd deal, even if that meant detention.

Could that mean detention?

So what, so what, so what, I chanted, with the rhythm of my pounding feet, my palms almost sweaty at the thought. I needed to focus on what had just happened to me—what *was* happening to me. The reality of that turned my run into a prance as I crossed the rest of the lot. Only, as I wove out from behind the last car, I froze.

Hawk Taylor was sitting on the steps, and I was pretty sure he'd caught me prancing, judging by his crooked smile.

Of all the people.

"Is Miss Valedictorian late for school?" he asked.

I relaxed from my just-caught-prancing pose and tried to ignore the final bell blaring its disapproving tone. Funny how it didn't sound so judgmental when you were on the other side of it.

"It's Billie who'll be valedictorian," I corrected.

He squinted up at me. "Same difference."

Same difference? He couldn't differentiate between me and my best friend?

I frowned at the double doors behind him. The halls were calling me, but the girl in the mirror was begging me to prove him wrong. Sure, old Eden would hurry inside, knowing Hawk Taylor would never be interested in someone so concerned with tardiness or detention, but the new, perfect Eden would have the confidence to snag whoever she wanted.

With a decisive nod, I sat down next to him. "Why are you

choosing to be late, if you were already here?"

He leaned away from me a bit. "Why are *you*?"

"Good question." Forget being late for school, I wasn't the type of girl who would sit down next to someone I hardly knew. Not if it might be considered the first move.

Twisting the watch on my wrist, I remembered the image in the mirror—sanded down and polished to perfection. That girl could pull off cool and irreverent if she wanted to, wouldn't worry about sounding dumb, and would most definitely not yelp, jump up, and run into the school like I was having an urge to do.

I stood to face him, resting my fingers on the gold band of my watch, and forced myself to be a little daring. "I've been meaning to tell you how much I liked the poem you wrote, the one in the last school paper."

"Oh. Thanks." He nodded. "I'm on a smoke break."

"What?"

"You answered my question, so I answered yours."

"But you're not smoking."

"I'm just saying, that's what everyone thinks I'm doing. Really, I can't face homeroom. We're too old for that, don't you think?"

I let out an odd sort of mumble. I'd never thought about homeroom because I was the type of girl who accepted the status quo.

He smiled a little, probably about whatever noise had

gotten caught in my nose, but then said, "You look really nice today."

"I do?" *More proof.* I cleared my throat. "I do." With confidence this time. Because he saw it. And if he saw it, it was true. "You look really nice today, too." I guess this new me wasn't any smoother than the old me. Not that it mattered, because Billie was right. Hawk and I were on opposite ends of the high school spectrum. If cool sat in the middle, I was too good for it, too worried about my grades, and he was too... Well, he probably didn't give one crap about the high school spectrum.

He smirked. "Nice is not what I was going for."

I laughed, and then, instead of yesterday's Eden, who would think too long about what she should say until she missed her chance, I just said it: "Whatever you were going for, I like it."

Forcing myself to not look away, I bit my lip. What was I doing? I was late for school and might get detention, which would totally piss off my volleyball coach.

"You should be late for school more often," he whispered, his gaze dropping to my lips.

Of course he was looking at my lips. They were perfectly plump now. I could barely take my eyes or teeth or fingers off them either.

I wanted to ask him out. Should I ask him out? Where was Billie when I needed her? But she'd probably point out that even a one-night transformation couldn't make me into the kind of girl he dated. Nothing could do that.

Deflated, I tried to catch a glimpse of my new self—my better, more confident self—in the window, but this only reminded me how late I was. Swallowing all the excitement of the morning, I said, "I better go."

He nodded. "Of course."

Of course. Because no matter what I looked like, I was still only the shy, almost-valedictorian.

3

It took me until third period to realize Hawk might have been interested. He didn't smile at everyone like that, only the people close to him—only his best friend Ivy. And I'd missed my chance by walking away instead of saying what I wanted to say.

I should've asked him out. I should've used this perfect Eden while I had her. Rolling my eyes over to Billie, I mouthed, "I am such an idiot."

She was used to this commentary, since I was socially awkward regularly, so she knew exactly what I'd said. In response, she winked at me. She only started winking after her third energy drink of the day, and it was just after ten.

"You have a problem, have I told you that?" I asked, after the bell released us into the dingy high school hallway.

She skipped right over her energy drink addiction with: "Why are you an idiot this time?"

"Because I should've asked Hawk out this morning."

"Hawk Taylor?" She squinted at me a little. "I thought you were over that fool."

"He's not a fool. Did you read his last poem in the paper?"

She ignored me, because of course she hadn't. "You were late over someone who is probably failing senior year?"

I opened my mouth to tell her about the mirror, then realized how crazy it sounded. "Sort of."

"Poor Wes."

"No. No 'poor Wes'. He hasn't made any sort of move in months."

"Wes would be good for you," she said, as we arrived at my locker.

"*I* am already good for me. I need someone who *won't* be good for me."

"Since when do people go looking for things that won't be good for them?" She said this like she had all the answers. Unfortunately for me, she generally did. It was why I asked her about everything before I did it.

"So, you don't think I should ask him out?" Even though I knew the answer wouldn't be different the second time.

"Of course I don't think you should ask him out."

And that would normally seal the deal. Normally, I would feel better and agree. But his smile nagged at me, the way he'd given me his attention when most of the time he seemed like he wasn't paying attention to anything at all.

We were seniors, and I'd spent my life doing what my mom and best friend thought I should do, but pretty soon I'd have to make my own decisions, and I didn't want to look back and think I should have started now. Judging by what I'd collected of Hawk's lyrics and poems over the years, he was pretty amazing. If I listened to Billie, yet again, I might never get to experience that (him) for myself.

Unfortunately, I wasn't even sure how to not listen to her, at this point.

Collecting my hair to pull it over my shoulder, I realized it was still damp. It was lunch, almost halfway through the school day, and my hair wasn't dry.

More proof that it was thicker than yesterday. I might have to start blow-drying it.

Billie slammed my locker shut and headed for the cafeteria, but I pulled up the camera on my phone to check my hair, my fingers rifling through the strands until she came back to drag me along with her.

"Sorry, it's just... Do I look different to you?" Sliding my phone in my pocket, I posed for her. With a hip cocked out and hands on my waist, I tossed my thicker, more luxurious hair and batted my eyelashes.

"No. Why are you standing like Ivy?"

Yes, she was talking about that Ivy. Hawk's best friend. Ivy was a singer. She had her own band, which was pretty hard core. She was also super skinny, like a model, but the kind who are on runways and not the curvier ones who do lingerie.

"I'm going to take that as a compliment," I decided.

"I didn't mean it as a compliment."

"So? I can take it as one, if I want."

She narrowed her eyes a little. "You were posing like her, like when she's on stage and trying too hard. That's what I meant."

"I knew what you meant. But she's also skinny. Don't I look skinnier today?"

"It's not about being skinny, Eden. It's about conquering the world." She pointed to her t-shirt, which read, *A woman's place is in the House and the Senate.*

"Says Miss Valedictorian," I mumbled.

She kissed the air toward me. "And don't you forget it."

"But really. I didn't say anything before class because I wanted you to notice on your own."

"Notice what?"

I leaned closer to her as we walked. "Everything about me is better today," I whispered, feeling the change rise up in me again, jittery and electric. Like a live wire, like anything could happen—*like I could ask him out.*

"Are you feeling okay?" she asked.

Fine, so Billie wouldn't notice because she didn't believe beauty mattered. Because she had "principles" and more important things to worry about. But my mom and Reese had noticed. And Hawk had, too.

We made it to the lunch line and started down it with our trays. Billie took not one, but two energy drinks, and I immediately put them back on the shelf.

She gave me a look, but she needed to be cut off.

"Aren't you eating anything?" she asked.

We'd already passed the tater tots, brownies, and burgers,

all of which on a normal day would've ended up on my plate. Only, I didn't know how this perfect Eden thing worked. Could I shove my face with ice cream and not gain a pound? This might be my one chance to do it right.

"I think I'm going to have a salad today."

She shot me another look. "You do know how cranky you get when you eat salads, right?"

But I was smaller now, and maybe my stomach was too, so it's possible a salad would do. Just in case, I grabbed a fruit cup.

She raised her eyebrows but didn't say anything. We paid and found our table.

As I was bending over to sit down, Jonathon nodded in my direction. "Hey, Cheeks."

Though I hadn't heard this much since junior high, when I did it was usually accompanied by a snicker. Today, however, he said it in a whole new way. An appreciative kind of way.

I grinned for a second, until Billie's frown shut me up. "Asshat," she muttered.

"I think he meant it as a compliment."

"Regardless, he's an asshat."

I bit the inside of my cheek to keep from smiling again, and picked at my salad in a way I imagined Ivy might.

Ivy was the kind of girl who'd ask Hawk out. She definitely made her own decisions without asking anyone what they thought of them.

Isaac slammed down next to Billie, and Wes slid onto the

bench next to me.

"A salad?" Wes asked. "There's nothing good for me to pick off a salad."

He usually took my discards. And sometimes tried to sneak the even better stuff.

I grinned brightly. "Maybe that was my plan."

He nodded. "Effective."

"You have volleyball tonight?" Isaac asked me. Though Billie and I looked nearly identical (her hair a little lighter, mine a little curlier), Isaac was a significantly messier version of Wes. But only because Wes was so neat. He was so neat he might as well be wearing a suit and tie.

"Yes, I do."

"See, I told you she couldn't do it tonight," Wes said, before biting into his burger.

"Do what?"

"Our final swim."

"Oh, right."

Isaac had a huge pool in his backyard, the one we'd trained in together back when we were all on swim team. We wasted most of our summers there.

With a charmingly arrogant smile on his face, Isaac said, "I worked the State angle to get my parents to keep it open a bit longer."

Wes offered him a fist and they bumped knuckles. The two of them were serious swimmers and this was to be their year.

It was also supposed to be our year—the volleyball team's. Yay for seniors all around.

"What about Saturday after my performance?" Billie asked, as she broke up her soft pretzel into bite-sized pieces. Billie had given up swimming sophomore year for an open mic and a soap box.

"I have to babysit my brothers," Wes said.

"I'm free Sunday," I offered.

Wes glanced at me. We'd been studying on Sundays for as long as I could remember.

"Same," Billie said.

"Perfect." Isaac took a huge bite of his burger. "Sumday ih is."

~

I rushed down the hall on the way to practice, trying not to hit anyone with my massive backpack, when I spotted Hawk coming from the other direction.

Skidding to a halt as I reached him, I imagined saying it— *Will you go out with me?*—but he spoke first.

"You gonna have time for all that tonight?" He nodded to my bag.

"Of course." I dropped it on the ground to give my shoulder a break. "I make time for my homework."

"You say that like I don't." But he was smirking, which, to be honest, looked insanely good on him.

Caught up in his smile, or maybe his accurate assessment, not that I was being judgy—did it sound like I was being judgy?—my mouth only managed to flap open and shut a few times.

This was not going well. I should ask him out. But Billie's voice hung in my head: *No, you should not.*

Yes, I should.

But Javi and Nat showed up before I could, stepping right into our conversation like they'd been there the whole time. Javi, in her daily uniform of high-end leggings and crop tops, twists already collected in a low pony behind her so they wouldn't get in her face during practice, and Nat in her usual jeans and a hoodie with a messy top knot. Javi scooped up my bag while Nat slid her arm through mine and pulled me toward the locker room.

I shot Hawk an apologetic look and let them take me. After all, late to school was one thing, but late to volleyball was another. I was co-captain this year, which was as good as a job in my mom's book, so no matter what kind of girl I was, that was of utmost importance. Setting a good example for my brother had always been a thing, but now I was also supposed to set an example for the team.

"Is he your community project?" Nat asked, glancing back at Hawk as we turned the corner to enter the locker room.

"No! Why would you even say that?"

They shared a look.

"Haven't you read his stuff?" I asked. "And he's kind of cute, don't you think?"

Javi thought about this a moment, then nodded. "Okay, he's not ugly." She motioned me to turn around and started braiding my hair while I worked on Nat's. It was quicker than doing it ourselves.

"I was thinking of asking him out," I admitted, softer now so the rest of the team didn't hear.

Nat jerked her head to look at me, and I lost the braid I was plaiting. She mouthed *sorry* and resumed position. "What about Wes?"

"What about him?"

Javi sighed. "Your hair is so pretty."

"Since when?" My turn to jerk my head around, but it was long enough that she could still hang onto it. "Since this morning?"

"Since forever."

I turned back to finish Nat's hair. But Javi didn't say that regularly, so maybe she noticed something subconsciously. I grinned. I would ask Hawk out tomorrow, no matter what anyone had to say about it. Tomorrow would be the day when I did things. In fact, maybe I would do all the things I thought about doing, without running them by anyone else first.

This had me standing taller as we finished up and entered the gym.

Oh, the smell of the gym. The locker room might turn sour on a regular basis, but you could always count on the gym for that sweet inhale of rubber. In that breath, even if the space was empty, I could hear the echo of shoes squeaking, the promise of a great serve, the thrill of a winning game. Forcing my lungs to fill with as much air as possible, bigger and bigger until it almost hurt, I then exhaled to a grin.

I'd gotten sick of being one of four—and really, the least talented swimmer of us all. Making the volleyball team freshman year had been one thing I'd done that Billie advised against. It had been my grandpa who'd inspired me to try something new, to change it up a little for high school, to meet new people.

Well, I had, but it hadn't changed me. And I was sick of myself. Waking up the way I had this morning, though, had me feeling like it was time to finally be a new person. Maybe that's what Grandpa had been trying to tell me; maybe he'd been trying to push me out of my comfort zone. Yet still, I'd woken up perfect and hadn't done anything different. I imagined his face, if he could see me now. Not the frown like my mom doled out—Grandpa would never frown at me—but a wrinkled forehead of concern. Like I was wasting my chance. I determined that tomorrow, if it lasted, for both his sake and mine, I would do everything differently.

This was all spinning through my head during warm up and drills. Coach sauntered up as I bumped Javi's spike to Nat, who set it to Javi, and noted, "You seem kind of distracted today."

"I do?"

He nodded to Nat. "She had to take two steps to get to that one."

Nat looked at me and shrugged. "She could make me take three and I'd still get it."

"Well, she's better than that," he said, then walked away to critique someone else.

Javi tossed me the ball to get us started again, and as I hit it with a little more focus this time, Javi shouted, "You play how you practice!" Then she slammed the ball down, full force.

She was fierce, good enough to get a full ride to college. The rest of us were banking on volleyball to help our college applications stand out in the pile, but she was banking on it getting her there, period.

Where Billie was all about mental and emotional strength, Javi was all about physical. I glanced down at my watch, which I should've taken off for practice, just in time to get hit in the head by her next vicious spike.

Thursday

At least it hadn't been my nose. Javi had given Lucy two bloody noses already this year. The bump on my head still hurt the next morning, but was thankfully covered by my hair.

I sat up in bed, suddenly remembering that hair, and how it looked yesterday, wondering if it would still be like that today. Grabbing my clothes, I hurried down the hall to the bathroom, to the mirror.

Yes. *Yay.* Phew.

One more day, at least. A second chance. Maybe this wasn't a fluke. Maybe this new me was here to stay.

Biting down on the inside of my lip, I wondered if it was just that I'd lost weight—the lighter me making all my features seem bigger. I could go to Billie's after school and weigh myself, but would that challenge the magic?

Hopping into the shower, I decided I couldn't chance breaking the spell quite yet.

My mom had made oatmeal instead of eggs that morning, and when I sat across from her and my little brother, I decided against butter. Sugar was necessary in life, but butter only greased things up.

"Game tonight?" my mom asked. She liked to verify our evenings first thing in the morning, even though she knew better than the rest of us what was coming.

I nodded and tried to swallow the sticky oats. Okay, so greasing things up probably helped them go down a little easier.

Reese grinned. "I love Thursday nights."

A phone buzzed, and I glanced toward mine, sitting on the counter. It wasn't blinking though, and my friends wouldn't text me now unless it was important—they knew my mom was a stickler about no electronics at the table.

My mom, however, was suddenly working her cell with her thumbs.

"Mom!" I cried, trying to be as aghast as she would if I was on my phone at the breakfast table.

She tried to hide her smile, but it wouldn't be contained. And with the light streaming in through the window, it was definitely a moment to capture. I wish I had my phone; I'd take a picture.

Wait. I checked my watch. It wasn't even eight yet. "Who would be texting you at this hour?"

Flushed, she stuffed her phone back into her pocket. She

never kept her phone in her pocket. It was always in her purse, or on her nightstand.

"A friend." She picked her spoon back up. "Eat your breakfast."

A friend. Holy cow. A man friend, no doubt, judging by the smile that tugged at her cheeks. I gave her a pointed look, and she gave me one back that she'd probably learned from me.

"A *man* friend?" I asked. She hadn't dated since Grandpa died last year, and had only one serious boyfriend after she left my dad, a few years after Reese was born.

My brother shifted in his seat, face pinched.

"Reese, do you have to go to the bathroom?" Mom asked, as she went for her phone again.

He shook his head, still shoveling oatmeal into his mouth.

"Mom." I turned back to her. "Is that a man texting you?"

"Just a coworker."

"Mom!"

She glanced over to Reese and then back to me, which meant she wasn't bringing this man around until she was decided about him, and we should keep the whole thing on the down-low.

"Fine." I put my palm out for her phone. "But if I don't get to text at the table, then neither do you."

She laughed. "Though I accept your terms, I am not handing over my phone."

With the kind of raised eyebrow that made a point, I choked

my last bite of sticky oatmeal down and drained my OJ, only to realize I'd never be late at this pace. Rinsing my bowl multiple times before placing it in the dishwasher, I even wiped down the counter before heading back to my room for my bravest-looking pair of shoes.

I mean, if my mom was dating again, I could ask a guy out. Maybe it would be a big day for the Calloway family all around.

Armed with the kind of confidence that can only come from magic, I took the longest route to school. Which was pretty difficult, considering we lived across the street from the football field.

Managing to arrive moments after the bell, I was greeted with Hawk on the steps once again, as I'd hoped. This time I wasn't prancing, so my entrance was very cool. At least, until he offered me one of the two cups of coffee in his hands. Two cups; one for me. I almost stumbled in surprise.

Wicked sexy smile, check. Tilted head of amusement, check. All the colors of all the world lighting up my fluttering belly, check.

He ran a hand through his almost-blond hair, something he did regularly, which I knew because I'd watched him and also because it mostly stayed smoothed back as if it had been trained. His mouth was set at a natural pout, which gave him a serious sort of resting face, and with the way his eyebrows leaned in toward each other, one might describe him as intense.

I sighed. He was beautiful. I mean, I wouldn't tell him that or anything, seeing he wanted to be all punk or rock or whatever it was he wanted to be, but I thought he was beautiful. Mainly because it sounded nicer and more polite than damn hot.

My mom was big on polite.

I stood there too long, and he studied me. "Good morning?" he asked.

"Well, I'm hoping it will be," I admitted.

He nodded toward the cup. I took it and sat down, wrapping both hands around it. They weren't cold, but it was reflex.

He reached over to loosen my fingers, so I could see the words scribbled across the side:

The warmth of your hair
would calm a bitter night—
the depth of your eyes
set a hurricane right.

I stared at his scrawl and marveled at the kind of belly fluttering you hear about, but that had never happened to me in all the years of Wes.

"Will you go out with me?" I blurted. Not exactly smooth, but at least I did it. Still, you'd think with this perfect face and thick head of hair, I wouldn't be so nervous as to feel my knees tremble. I couldn't even look at him, not until he answered. If he said no, I'd force myself to. I'd smile, stand, and thank him for the coffee.

"I'd love that."

My gaze shot over, and he nudged my knee with his. Without thinking, I raised an eyebrow, because maybe he was just trying to clean up his reputation by rubbing arms with a smart rule-follower.

He chuckled. "You look like you don't believe me."

"I'm not sure I do."

"Read the poem again, Eden."

So I did. It was lovely. "I don't recognize it." Did that give away how I'd read everything he'd ever put out there?

"Because it's new." He stressed the word *new*. Then softer, he added, "Written just for you."

I about gaped at him. It felt like the air was tangled between us, caught up in what he was saying, as surprised as I was.

Hawk Taylor had written a poem for perfect Eden. I sat in that for a moment. Then, taking a deep breath in, I settled into this person I was going to be today. This person who would *do* things and not think twice. This new me.

"When?"

Letting out a slow grin, he replied, "Tonight."

Tonight was a school night. A Thursday. Plus, "I have a game."

"After your game. I'll take you to my favorite diner."

I reminded myself that I wasn't the type of girl anymore who cared what night it was. And our games were usually over by eight. I could shower at school, not that I wanted to get ready for a first date in a stinky locker room, but I didn't really want my mom to meet him yet, either. She might be surprised she hadn't heard about him, and the fact that it happened so fast wouldn't go down very well. She thought people should be friends first. She thought Wes and I were a great fit.

"Meet me in the hall outside the locker room. I'll have to shower, but I'll be quick."

He grinned. "Well, this is turning out to be a good morning for me. What about you?"

I nodded. But even for this new me, it was almost too much, so I studied the long curves of his handwriting, the pattern his words made against the cross-grain of the coffee cup. Like a kaleidoscope.

He checked his watch and I grabbed for his wrist, again without thinking about it.

Commit, I told myself, refusing to recoil and instead letting my fingers linger. "Your watch looks ancient," I muttered.

"It was my uncle's. Old stuff speaks to the poet in me."

I offered him my wrist. "My grandma's."

He tapped his watch to mine, like a toast. "To old stuff."

With a grin, I dared say, "And new." *Yes! I did it. See, I can do it!*

"And new," he repeated, then cleared his throat. "Are you going to finish your coffee?"

"I guess, if you're going to have another cigarette."

This got a laugh out of him, which was encouraging. I relaxed a little bit.

"Why does everyone assume that's what you're doing?" I asked. "Did you just quit or something?"

"It's just what people assume, moody outcast that I am."

"You aren't an outcast."

"Oh, but I am."

"Because you want to be."

"Maybe. Maybe both. Maybe because I want to *and* because people assume. The chicken or the egg, which came first?"

"The chicken."

"You sound very certain."

"I am very certain."

We stared at each other for an intense pause.

He broke it first, his tone soft and low. "The girl or the wonder, Miss Girl Wonder?"

"The girl," I replied, not missing a beat. He nodded once, and I didn't confess that the Wonder had just shown up yesterday.

"The girl will be absent if she doesn't scurry."

I raised an eyebrow at him. "Scurry?"

He shrugged. "I play with words. It's what I do."

With a smile, I lifted the coffee cup. "Thank you for this."

He looked at it, face serious, then at me. "After your game?"

I nodded. And in case there was any doubt, I said it, too: "I'll be there."

5

The team that night should've been an easy win. Plus, I was perfect, so that should have made it even easier. At least, that's what I told myself at the start of the game, when I was high on game-day popcorn fumes. Then I'd missed my serves, botched a set, and got lectured at half time.

Was it because Hawk was there? I'd noticed him while searching the stands for my mom and Reese, but I'd still felt focused.

Javi elbowed me as we walked back onto the court, though. "Focus, Calloway."

Right. I rolled my neck and shoulders, swung my arms a few times, then got into position. I was perfect today, and perfect meant domination on the volleyball court. Just look at my senior banner hanging between Javi and Nat's on the far end of the gym. We'd agreed on no smiles. Serious, like the boys' banners always were. Arms crossed, all business, implying not just domination, but dominion.

Javi's first two serves were over in a blur. She and I were the stars when it came to serving, and yet I'd barely made one of mine tonight. That was almost as bad as Nat's overhand stats, which she compensated for with her blocking record.

I jumped around a little to shake the thoughts from my

brain. I needed confidence if I was going to turn this around. The ball came at me, a volley off Javi's third serve, but I wasn't ready for it. I was two seconds behind its trajectory, which meant I couldn't back up fast enough, and it did that awful humiliating smack in the crook of my elbows instead of landing on my forearms where it was supposed to.

My teammates all groaned, knowing Javi's serves would be another full rotation around, and we'd likely lose by then. Coach set his clipboard and whistle down to cross his arms, which was pretty much his tell for having given up.

After that, it was all over. It'd been hard enough shirking my own insecurities, but everyone else's disappointment? There wasn't enough time to make up for it.

We lost the game and I couldn't help but feel like it was my fault. Lining up to congratulate the other team, I hugged my free arm around my belly and got ready to eat the smirks off our opponents' faces. Yep, I would do my duty and collect them all on my own. No need for anyone else, who'd put in their full effort and skill, to have to deal with that.

"Are you okay?" Javi whispered from behind me, as we held out our hands and slap, slap, slapped our way down the line. It was like a train on tracks, the steady bump of humiliation in the face of what you hadn't done, and you couldn't get off until the end of the line.

I hid behind Nat as Coach stood in front of us, his mustache moving a bit here and there, but not enough to get his mouth moving. It was excruciating. Then, finally, "I think I said all I needed to say at half time."

As I hurried away, though, he called after me. Nat and Javi swept me swiftly into the locker room, where he wouldn't go, even for a scolding.

If he was going to yell at me, it didn't need an audience. Plus, I'd yelled at myself enough as it was, and I didn't have time. I had a date to get ready for.

He called for me once again, and Nat sighed. "I'll go tell him you're dealing with some serious womanly cramps."

"No!" I cried, turning to catch her. "Not true. And don't use that. Not cool."

She squinted at me a little. "Why not use what you can?"

"No." Billie was in my head, shaking a fist at how it was these kinds of things that set us back. *Using what we can.* Never, if it wasn't actually true. And if it was, take some painkillers, for goodness' sake.

She raised her hands. "Fine, I'll tell him you have a date to get ready for and you're having second thoughts." Spinning on her heel, she muttered, "Because that's so much better."

I looked at Javi. "I'm not having second thoughts."

"I saw him. He shaved for you. It helps."

I would've beamed if I wasn't so busy wincing about the most pathetic game I'd just played. I'd left my watch on, for magic's sake, twisting it upside down under my long sleeve jersey so it wouldn't be noticeable. *Dumb*, I reminded myself.

There was no such thing as magic. That being said, I didn't have it in me to test it. It had showered with me a few times already, and it would again.

Had I merely been distracted during the game, or was it that since I wasn't as thick, I wasn't as strong? Focus was one of my strengths; I didn't usually get distracted. And I'd been puffing after ten minutes, which was kind of ridiculous.

Being delicate shouldn't make me soft, but what if that's how it was going to play out for me? What if I had to trade big and strong for small and weak? Old me or new me—physically strong but shy and timid, or physically weak but confident and bold?

On one hand, the old me had gotten this far: varsity volleyball, salutatorian, and early admission plus some necessary prospects for great scholarships. On the other, the old me didn't have it in her to step out of her comfort zone or be anyone but what she *should* be. I wanted to be what I *wanted* to be, and, as an aside, I wanted Hawk. The old me couldn't get him, either.

Nat was back and gone by the time I was out of the shower, so I texted her a thank you, that I owed her, kissy faces and the like, then made my way to get dressed, dried, and made-up. When I swung through the now empty locker room and out to the hall, Wes was alone in the dim corridor.

"Here I thought you'd be moping all night," he said.

I sucked a little on my lower lip, which got me wondering if maybe Hawk would do the same later, which got me feeling guilty about Wes, who, come to think of it, was usually waiting for me after my games to take me to wherever our friends were. And there I went, nearly gagging on my own spit.

Crap, I never told him...

He furrowed his brow. "You all right?"

"I, uh, have a date tonight."

He sent me a loose grin. "That's what we're finally calling it?"

"Calling what?"

Offering his elbow, he said, "I knew you'd eventually come around."

"What are you talking about?"

He dropped his arm. "Us. I'm talking about us."

I shook my head. "I told Billie I wasn't going with you guys. I have other plans."

"Wait." He put up a finger. "You mean you have a date with someone else?"

I flushed. "Is that so hard to believe?"

Wes stared at me like I'd just burned every bunny there'd ever been. "With who?"

"Hawk Taylor."

"Hawk?" It was almost a laugh. As if Wes never thought Hawk would go for me. Because I, metaphorically speaking, wore shiny perfect shoes I would never let get dirty.

It pissed me off. "I'm not kidding."

His brow furrowed, and I inhaled a whiff of his mint-scented shampoo. Salon shampoo and ironed clothing, pool-formed muscles and the classic movies his mom made him watch, that's what Wes was made of. There was nothing wrong with wanting to try out slugs and snails and puppy dog tails. So what if my shoes got a little dirty? Maybe it was time.

Hawk's footsteps sounded out before he rounded the corner, so both Wes and I were staring at him when he did.

"You're not kidding," Wes muttered, with as much oomph as the last bit of air draining from a balloon.

I brushed past him.

Hawk's face was curious, but he went with it, setting his hand on my back and guiding me forward, away from Wes.

Wes, who would never be so bold as to guide me anywhere.

6

How do you tell a person you don't like them?

Worse yet, how do you tell one of your oldest friends you don't like them? At least, not like that.

It was always a nice thought, Wes and I, but that was it— nice. And I hadn't wanted to ruin what the four of us had. Though now I very well might have.

These thoughts made our ride to the diner silent and awkward. Great job, Eden.

As Hawk and I slid into opposite sides of a lime green booth, I futzed with my watch, reminding myself I was now delicate and petite, which translated to bright and confident.

Forcing out a smile, I said, "I hope that wasn't the first game you've come to."

He gave me a wrinkled look. "Yeah, you didn't play your best."

"So not your first?" I asked hopefully.

"Well, yes, actually. But I do walk the halls and hear things."

"What things do you hear?"

He smiled. "That you, Nat, and Javi make the team what it is."

Trying to avoid a blush, I looked out the window at the large *D* in *DINER* behind him. It was pretty cool, the peach neon glow making his profile crisper. I pulled my phone out to take a picture.

I liked making what I saw even more beautiful than it was in real life, with the right tilt or lighting or filter.

After loading it up, I turned my phone to him so he could see and tag himself if he wanted. Then I'd have his user name and could follow him. "Nat and I are only the favorites because Javi picked us," I admitted. "Javi's the star."

He clasped his hands in front of him on the table. "Can I be frank?"

More words that had me nervous and unsettled. Great. I turned my screen off and set it face down on the table. On second thought, I moved it onto the seat next to me. Out of sight. "Please."

"The halls also speak of you and Wes. Which I didn't think much of when you asked me out, but after seeing you two tonight..."

I swallowed the truth of those halls, of what I felt I was fighting against. "Those halls do really talk a lot."

He smiled, a bit sadly. "They do."

First date etiquette faux pas by Eden Calloway, part two (or was it three?): talk about another guy in the first fifteen minutes.

But, he'd asked. We were being frank. I sighed. "Wes kissed me once, a while back. I didn't think too much about it, because it never happened again. What you saw was me telling him I had a date, and him thinking it had to be with him, because who else would go out with me?"

"Well, me, for one."

"Yes, that's what I told him."

His sad smile was kind now. "He probably listens too much to those halls and didn't think we'd be a good match."

In a flash of chance and goodwill, I managed not to drop my mouth open and blurt out, *No one does, do you?*

Maybe this was only because I was saved by the waitress, who swooped in like a phantom. "Hi, dears. What can I do you for?"

"Coffee. Black," Hawk said. She then winked at him, and he winked back. So when she turned to me and didn't wink, the new me dared to wink at her.

"Cola. Ice."

Hawk laughed and she raised her eyebrows. "You got a spitfire here, Baby."

"I know, Mom."

"Mom?" I gawked at them. Suddenly she was more than a nice lady in a white button-down dress with a peach-checkered apron and collar. Suddenly her bushy brown hair and dark cherry lipstick were colored in, and those eyelashes—were they real? There wasn't a drop of makeup on her face aside from her mouth, but those lashes nearly reached for me.

"This is Eden Calloway. Eden, my mother."

I crossed my arms and laid my head on them with a groan.

It didn't matter at this point. I'd already ruined the first impression.

She patted my shoulder. "Don't worry, hon. I'm kind of a spitfire myself. In fact, I think I'll bring you guys some fries, on the house."

I took a deep breath before sitting up, but she was gone as fast as she'd come. "That was not fair."

He busted out in laughter and that alone made me smile. "You keep surprising me."

I groaned. "With my bad manners?"

"I just can't guess which way you're going to go."

Me neither, I wanted to say. How observant. Caught between two people and two choices at every turn, that's how I felt, even though I thought I'd committed to one that very morning. I guess there was a learning curve for everything, even being a new me.

"Did you like my picture?" I asked.

He nodded. "I like all your pictures; I just don't press like buttons."

"But, you don't follow me, do you?"

"In fact, I do."

"You do?" I tried my hardest not to glance down at my phone, but I did let my fingers run over its case.

"I've been following you forever, you just never followed me back. I figured it was because you thought I was such a slacker."

42

I really wanted to get back to him liking my pictures, because that was a glowing, big ball of happy inside my chest, but instead I committed once again to the bold new me. "Slacker or not, I've had a little thing for you for ages."

It was the first time I'd seen him falter, and I grinned. Like a stutter or stammer, but visual, it took him a moment to collect himself. "I'm not really a slacker."

"You let people think you are."

"I can't control what people think."

I mirrored his posture, and decided I might want his brain, if he truly didn't care what people thought or worry about what actions of his might reinforce their judgments.

"Just because I skip class doesn't mean I'm not getting my work done. Just because I don't like sitting through long-winded lectures doesn't mean I need a cigarette. And just because I vape once in a while doesn't mean I'd do so on school grounds. People draw their own lines; that's on them."

Hawk's mom slipped our order on the table so fast I didn't have time to say thank you.

"How does she do that?"

"*Why* does she do that," he corrected. "She does it because I yell at her for intruding on my dates."

"Then why would you bring them here?"

"To see a side of me that they might take seriously."

I crossed my hands in front of me on the table. "Can I be frank?"

He chuckled a little and bit into a fry. "Please."

"Explain."

"That's not exactly being frank."

I popped two fries into my mouth. "Then you do the being frank with your explanation."

His turn to sigh, and now it felt like we were back on the same playing field. "Everyone thinks I'm just in it for, well, you know—"

I grinned. "Nope, I don't. And you are to be frank, remember?"

He hung his head. "Everyone thinks I just want to sleep with them, but that's not true. I'm actually kind of a romantic."

"I know." I grabbed my phone for another picture, this time the D on top of him. "Anyone paying attention to what you write should know that."

He peeked up. "Thank you for saying so."

I nodded.

"Thank you for paying attention."

I smiled and shifted in my seat. Then ate a fry.

"Girls use me that way a lot. To piss off a boyfriend, or an ex. Or because they're bored, but not because they actually like me." He leaned back in the booth. "Where do you think I get all the inspiration for my poems?"

"Well, I thought that was from me."

With a grin, he pulled a pen out of his back pocket, grabbed a napkin, and scribbled on it, hiding his words with his other hand. It didn't take him long to finish, straighten up, and slide it over:

The scent of your skin,
your hand gripped in mine—
we dissolve darkness,
catch, link, and entwine.

I blinked a few times, read it a few more, then set my fingertips on the ink that was both messy-boy writing and graceful poet script.

Folding the napkin, I tucked it into my purse and took a long drink of soda.

"That stuff will kill you," he said.

"So will your smoking," I retorted.

He grinned. "Wanna get out of here?"

Only if it means I can suck on your lip. But I didn't say that. One, because it was ridiculous, compared to his words, and two, because his mom probably would've shown up to hear it.

7

At the end of the road that the diner was on, the busy streets tapered off to a gas station. Beyond that was a tree-lined lane which ended at a parking lot, the bay stretching out beyond it.

A cracked shed to the right provided the only light hanging from its eave, and in front of us, along the shore, ran a thin row of weeping willows.

Hawk headed across the blacktop, onto a path obstructed by a permanent road block—the metal kind that swings back and forth for utility vehicles. It wasn't chained and didn't look hard to slide past, but it still announced that not just anyone was supposed to wander through.

After a few feet, he glanced back. "You coming?"

I had made it out of the car and got a creepy picture of the corners of the shed, peeling and folding like the wrinkles on a person's skin. Slipping my phone into my back pocket, I pointed at the barricade.

"People do this all the time," he assured.

What people? Glancing back at the empty lot, where the weeds were struggling their way through the cracks, I wondered how much traffic it could honestly get. But he was almost out of sight and it was creepier alone—the crumbling shed now more foreboding than fascinating.

I hurried after him until the trees thinned on our right, revealing the rippling glass of the bay, and thickened on our left, making it feel like we were in northern Wisconsin and not right at the edge of the city. That was the nice thing about the lakes that dotted our state; the city often had to give way for nature, there was no choice in the matter.

As I caught up, he offered me his hand for the first time, and just after having said that his hand linked in mine would dissolve darkness—catch, link, and entwine.

I reached for his fingers, and we both paused at the contact. His palm was rough, his finger pads rougher. He looked up at me, then started walking.

We stopped at the tip of a tiny peninsula. The moonlight bounced off the water and cast a soft glow toward us, calming the shadows and clearing the shapes. Hawk stepped onto one of the rocks that hugged the shore: flat ones and round ones and huge ones and small ones. You could probably get six feet out and not get wet, if you were careful. Looking back, he took a few steps forward, but only as far as he could go without letting go of my hand.

"Wanna dance?" he asked.

"I don't dance." Oh, that old me was hard to shake. "Maybe."

"No one's watching."

"You're watching."

"I'll be inside it, I can't watch."

I pulled my jacket tighter around me. "Jump around a little.

Make sure you're steady."

"Oh, I'm steady. The question is if you are."

But that was my problem. I was *too* steady.

This thought clanked around inside my brain, louder than anything else, so when I didn't say anything more, he dropped my hand and went hopping from rock to rock, skipping over the pointier and smaller ones. When he hit one that gleamed slick and slippery, I rushed forward until my toes tipped a baby boulder.

"No need to show off," I said, wishing he'd just stop moving.

"It's not deep here." He straddled two rocks, and the water rushed between his feet, easy waves pulsing back and forth. "This would probably be the best place to fall in."

"But you might hit your head on the way down."

"More like scrape a knee."

"Or break an arm." Paranoia, I know. I was the careful kind of girl, too. *Stop it. Not tonight.*

"Honestly, it's a great night for a swim. If we went in on purpose, then there'd be no threat of falling."

I choked out a laugh. "You're kidding, right?"

"Not even a little bit."

"You know it's September." I was planning on swimming at Isaac's on Sunday, but that would be in the sunshine at least, and in a heated pool.

It looked like he was trying to control a smirk. Probably because I was so rigid. "I do."

"We also don't have suits."

He chuckled, no controlling that.

"Hawk Taylor!" He didn't expect me to go skinny dipping on a first date, did he?

"Bras and undies are as modest as most bikinis," he said innocently, before sprouting a wicked sexy smile. "Why, what were you thinking?"

"I don't wear bikinis."

"Like, on principle?"

But it wasn't principle. I could say it was, but it would be Billie's words. My mom's. What were my words? Mine were about being too self-conscious and hiding behind the principle. Hiding behind my mom and Billie.

I stood a little taller. "If I had a suit, I'd go swimming." Even this new me was not comfortable enough to do so in a bra and underwear.

"Why don't you wear a bikini? Just curious."

"Why don't you wear a Speedo?"

He snickered. "How do you know I don't?"

"No way do you wear a Speedo."

"You wear a bikini, and I'll wear a Speedo."

"I'd have to go buy one."

"Same."

But, to answer his question, since I was all about bold and confident, and to me that meant telling the truth, I said, "I feel like I'd fall out of a bikini."

"Well, if it were too big, anyone would fall out of a bikini."

"I mean more like…"

He took a step forward. "You'd look good in anything."

"What about an ape suit?" I asked, without missing a beat. *Yay me.*

"HOT."

We both smiled, and with his eyes on me instead of watching where he was placing his feet, he moved slowly back in my direction.

Studying the flat boulder in front of me, I tested it with one foot, lifting my weight up a few times. Satisfied it didn't rock or sink, I committed at the same time Hawk landed on it from the other side.

He reached for my arms to stabilize us, while I looked up from our feet, which were nearly toe to toe. The water lapped softly and the breeze rustled gently, but all of it faded because being so close was that distracting. And his gaze… He was completely focused on my eyes, then my lips, then my eyes.

Then my lips.

Leaning down while guiding me towards him, he kissed me, tentative at first. As I accepted and responded, his caution faded. An arm slid behind me. Fingers wove through my hair. A shudder shook my spine.

Catch, link, and entwine.

I'd never before felt such a strong attraction to a person's mouth.

He pulled away and I sighed. With that smirk-turned-sexy grin, he tugged at my hand until we were both sitting on a rock. I ran my hand along the smooth surface as he leaned back a little to rest his palms behind him. "You dance on the volleyball court."

"What?"

"It's a dance, like anything else—moving your body toward something. With dance, it's a feeling, a mood, and with volleyball, it's a point, or a win."

"But I'm confident on the court." And I wasn't in life. It hit me then, how much stronger I felt with Javi and Nat when we played, all our strengths working together, versus the rest of my life where I what? Led with my weaknesses? Or simply let other people lead?

Leaning forward, I picked at the fraying hem of my jeans. Hawk's hand came over my fidgety fingers and wrapped them in a cocoon, holding them still and warm and safe.

"What else makes you feel confident?" he asked.

"You don't ask easy questions, you know that?"

"Well, in fairness, easy questions don't get you anywhere new."

I sighed. My 4.4 grade point average made feel strong and confident, and the way my little brother looked at me. But it felt fake, because on my own—without the immediate bolster of Reese's adoration, and who I thought I might be *in the future*—I didn't really ever feel like that, off the court.

At least not until I'd woken up perfect. Then I'd felt a hint of it. A wisp of a tendril I needed to somehow figure out how to keep hold of.

"Tell me what you like to do then," he asked. "If you don't like to swim and dance."

But it wasn't that I didn't *like* to. It was that I felt too self-conscious. So essentially, I ruined my own enjoyment of things. I stood up. "It's getting close to my curfew. We should probably head back."

He didn't say anything as we made our way to the parking lot, and I bit at my bottom lip, worried I'd ruined the magic by sliding back into my old self again.

He took a deep breath. "I'm sorry if—"

I hopped in front of him before he could finish his sentence. He shouldn't be apologizing. He hadn't said no to almost everything tonight. He hadn't avoided questions asked in an effort to get to know me better. But the only way to explain that was to apologize for the old me, still here between us.

What mattered more was proving to myself that whoever I was, I could be who I wanted. And if I couldn't do it today, when I looked perfect, when I'd promised myself I would, then I'd never be able to.

Stepping into him, I rested my lips on his, soft at first and then like I meant it, no reservations. Like this was a regular thing—me taking control and kissing people I wanted to kiss. I wanted to *feel* like it was a regular thing.

I kept his bottom lip in my mouth for a second, just to see, before I pulled away. But when I let go, he came into me again for more. He wasn't only certain this time, but tantalizing, and even a bit determined. Funny how you could sense all that in a kiss.

We were breathing heavily as I stumbled back next to him. Silent, and maybe for lack of what else to do, we started walking again. Our feet shuffled along the gravel, loud in the heavy silence.

As we approached the road block, Hawk cleared his throat. "So, how 'bout we do this again tomorrow?"

I smiled. "I have to go to the boys' swim meet, but Saturday Billie does this one-woman thing at the community theater. Totally amateur, sort of like an open mic. Wanna come?"

"Yes." His voice was solid and resolute as he grabbed for my hand. "Then there's this band—you know Ivy?"

I nodded. Everyone knew Ivy, even if they didn't *know her* know her.

"She's in this band and they play every Saturday night. Maybe we could go there after. You could meet her and some of the guys?"

"You have guys?" I teased, shoving my shoulder into him. "But you're such a loner."

"Only at school," he said, glancing over at me. "But now I have you."

Saturday

I woke up Saturday with a mission. The next step of Transformation Eden was to find a bikini I could stand, so Billie and I were at the mall, flipping through the clearance racks.

"What about this one?" she asked, pulling out a tankini.

"I told you, *bikini.*" Billie was having a much harder time with this than I was.

"You said two-piece." She pulled out another one, something halfway between a tankini and a bikini.

"*Bikini,*" I sang.

"Bikinis only further objectify the female body."

"Male bodies are objectified these days, too."

"That doesn't make it better. It's bad to objectify anyone, male or female."

I rolled my eyes, but so she couldn't see. "Anyway, it doesn't have to be a string bikini." I held up another for her, a green one. "What about this?"

She surveyed my chest, then the swimsuit, then back to my chest. "I do like the pattern. And it does have moderate coverage. That's a maybe."

"It's like I'm shopping with my mother."

She stuck her tongue out at me. "You used to agree."

Hm. Well, I can see how she thought that. But being me, separate from her, meant being honest instead of agreeing, right? Right. I took a deep breath. "I used to sort of agree—it shouldn't be my problem if a guy can't look at me without seeing an object. That should be his problem."

I pulled out another one, lifting it up for approval. She nodded, but I couldn't get over the ruffle so I put it back.

She threw her hands up. "Why ask if you're not even going to listen to me?"

Indeed. Maybe I needed to stop asking. "I'm sorry you're having such a hard time with this, Mom." I grinned at her. "But I want to try on someone new for a bit."

She braced her hand on the rack. "What's wrong with being yourself?"

What's wrong is I didn't know if I *had* been being myself, because I'd been in her shadow for so long. But I wasn't going to say that, not even if I were being me.

"Is this about Hawk?" she asked.

I absentmindedly flipped through the rack. "He said he'd wear a Speedo if I wore a bikini."

She frowned. "Gross. You're doing this to see him in a

Speedo?"

"No, because it's funny." I looked up and laughed. "They have to have those in clearance, right? I'm totally getting him one."

She wrinkled her nose. "You've been on one date. You are not buying him a gift after one date."

I stared at her, feeling the crossroads—the tug of old me veering to her wisdom, versus new me yanking the reins toward the road I wanted to head down. It was funny. He *would* laugh. And I would be more comfortable in a bikini if he were in a Speedo.

Plus, I was *not* Billie Same Difference. Not anymore.

"I one hundred percent am. The cheapest one."

She frowned again and this time I got that it wasn't the image of him in a Speedo. It was sadder than that. Not sure I wanted to open that can of worms, I just looked at her.

Of course, I should've known that Billie Wright would always open the can herself.

"You know this is going to change everything, right?"

"Change what?"

"The four of us."

"It doesn't have to. Wes and I were friends before he wanted to be anything else. He's dated other girls, and I've dated other guys, and that never changed things."

"This is our senior year, Eden."

"Point?"

But for once, she was quiet. Thinking. Because I'd finally disagreed with her?

"Are you saying I should date him because it's what he wants?" I asked.

But of course she couldn't say that. "Hawk won't fit the way your other boyfriends have."

"How do you know?" I almost dared her to say he wasn't smart enough, because he was, he just didn't flaunt it. Or that he wasn't good enough, but it's not like he'd ever been in real trouble, as far as I knew, so just because he wasn't cookie cutter? Well, I appreciated that, because I wanted to cut my own damn cookie for once.

"I guess I don't." She sighed, and it felt like she was expelling the tension of the entire conversation, like she was backing off and giving me this one. "Okay, so you should know something about me."

I prodded her with my bikini-laden hand.

"I own a two-piece." She put her hands up. "My mom bought it for me last year. But it still has tags on it."

Of course her mom bought it for her. She was as frilly as Billie was not. I laughed.

"I'd give it to you, but that one you'd definitely fall out of." She motioned a circle around her chest area. "Right into Hawk. Which is apparently not what you're going for?"

Gathering my choices, a peachy orange-red, a patterned green, and a shiny but smoky turquoise, I led her to the dressing rooms. "No, no immediate seduction necessary."

"Eventual seduction, though. Your boobs, in that, he will not forget." Mumbling into her hand, she added, "Sexual objectification."

I tossed the hanger over the door in the general vicinity of her voice. "I want to see that bikini of yours next time I'm over. Got it?" Actually not appalled with what I saw, I opened the door with a smile.

Billie stared at me with a pretty decent poker face while she walked over and attempted to stuff my breasts into the what-had-looked-wide-enough-on-the-hanger tube top.

I swatted her hands away. "Okay, Grandma."

"I don't like that color anyway, try the blue one." She raised her voice as I closed the door behind me. "So how exactly did Hawk and you end up talking about bikinis?"

"He asked me to go swimming, you know, when we were walking out by the bay. I, naturally, was appalled—"

"Naturally."

"And he said my bra and undies were as much coverage as a bikini."

"Clearly he hasn't seen your grandma panties."

Another hanger, and this time a direct hit. "Ow!" she cried, and then it came back over to me, clanged against the metal edge of the mirror, and tumbled to the floor.

I opened the door. "This one might be it."

Narrowing her eyes like she was studying something, she

walked over and yanked at the string on my hip.

"Billie!" I caught it before the bottoms could drop to my knees.

With a shrug, she turned to sit back down. "You should get that one, in case you decide on immediate seduction."

"So you're okay with immediate seduction, just not bikinis."

"Obviously."

I went back to the dressing room.

"You seducing means you're in charge," she explained. "Though, the fact that you're using your body to get what you want is problematic."

"Just because I'm in a bikini doesn't mean I'm no longer in charge," I pointed out.

"No, but essentially you're self-objectifying because you're so brainwashed into believing you must lead with your looks, thus it all comes back to *furthering the objectification of the female body.*" I said the last bit with her and the first hanger I'd thrown came sailing back at me.

"You know, this is good," she muttered. "I should be taking notes."

"Speaking of notes," I called over the partition, "a good way to find out if Hawk would fit in would be you and Isaac coming to see Ivy after your show tonight."

"Except, Ivy plays in a bar."

"Hawk says he can get us in."

"I feel like you're proving my earlier point."

Staring at the jade green suit in the mirror, letting the sight of a perfect fit fill me, plus the luxurious hair if I did say so myself, and the eyelashes for days, and the model's nose...

"He would spend the night in a bar," she explained. "We would not."

I turned from the mirror and put my fingers on the handle, but didn't want to face her, knowing what a big ask it was. I closed my eyes. "Please? I'd feel so much better if you were there." Then I bit my lip, because that was exactly the crutch I was trying to get out from under. Okay, so I wouldn't ask again. I wouldn't beg.

She didn't answer. And didn't answer. Could she see my feet, waiting?

"Of course I'll go. Though I'm morally opposed, I'm more morally opposed to being a crummy friend and leaving you hanging."

I grinned and flung the door open, strutting out with a model's walk, a spin, and a pose. Screw sexual objectification. Or if not, then at least I would own it.

Billie seemed to have thrown her ideals out temporarily too, as she was grinning and nodding her head so hard her bronze waves were bobbing. "I love it."

I did too. But more than that, I loved how it made me feel.

Like I was daring to be bold. Like I was daring to be myself.

9

Hawk parked in the back alley next to a navy van with a spattering of hand-painted stars, then proceeded to introduce me while the band unloaded their stuff.

It was good they were distracted, because I was too busy eyeing the backside of the bar we were about to sneak into to remember names or look at faces.

I knew Ivy from school, of course, not that I'd talked to her a ton since our Teen Cuisine restaurant project in eighth grade, where we'd been paired as assistant managers, but she picked up right where we'd left off, so I made sure to nod at her like I was listening, rather than gape at how relaxed she was.

We were not twenty-one. We were not allowed in bars. This was legit illegal. On top of buying a bikini that morning, it almost seemed like too much for one day. My head was about to explode.

Where were Billie and Isaac? They were supposed to have followed us from Billie's thing, and I couldn't do this without her. What had Hawk said on the way over? I didn't remember because I'd been looking out the windows, a turtle with its head tucked, as we wound downtown into the depths of the city where an unchaperoned seventeen-year-old probably shouldn't be.

Did everyone know there was a strip club on the corner of Main and 7th?

I soon spotted them; they must have parked on the street. Hawk looked at me, waiting for me to introduce them to the band, but I only blinked at him so he did the honors. Isaac was frowning—I knew he didn't approve—but Billie was shaking hands and being as courteous as ever.

We started to move, all of us at once, toward the door like we were going to open it and enter an establishment that served alcohol, and my hair stood on end. I reached up to check that it hadn't actually happened.

Ivy strode in first like she owned the place, and Hawk dipped his head toward mine. "Are you okay?"

"Trying not to draw any attention," I whispered.

He chuckled. "It's cool. There's no need to be nervous."

"Who said I was nervous?"

He bit back what I was sure was a smirk, shook hands with a guy holding a clipboard as we filed through, and ran his fingers through his messy blond hair as we walked down a dimly lit hall. Maybe he was a tiny bit nervous too. Or maybe it was just a general tic.

The band took a right into a room without a door, and we rounded a corner to the left, ending up in the packed bar.

I breathed a sigh of relief. For some reason, I thought we'd be the first here, and obviously underage, sticking out like Reese's cowlick on a bad day. This I could handle a little better.

Still, I slid my hand into Hawk's as he led us, Billie and Isaac behind me, to one of the few empty tables left. Hawk grinned at me, squeezed my hand, then turned to Billie.

"Impressive, your show. I like what you said about straws."

"Thanks. They *are* completely unnecessary."

He leaned forward a little. "And you really think those other countries just take our money and dump our plastic in their cities?"

"I don't think it. I know it. They really need to give me a projector. People don't listen to numbers; they listen to what they can see."

"I'm sorry. Listening is usually my strength. What were the numbers again?"

"Half the plastic made is trash within a year, and every year, five grocery bags of that trash for every foot of coast around the world ends up in the oceans." She paused to let this sink in. "The most quoted statistic is that by 2050, there will be more plastic in the oceans than fish, ton for ton."

"Well, I'm done." He threw up his hands. "Convinced. No more plastic for me if I can help it. And definitely no more straws."

Well, good for them. I was ecstatic they were getting along. But how could they think straight in a bar knowing we were underage?

Isaac rolled his eyes over to me, but I couldn't tell if we were sharing a heard-it-all-before-and-a-million-too-many-times or a what-the-hell-are-we-doing-here look.

That's when I realized I was acting like the me I didn't want to be. The one who did what Billie thought was best, and who was as scared as Isaac of getting in trouble—though he'd never admit it was fear. He wanted you to believe it was because he was morally opposed to doing the wrong thing. He worshipped order, and rules, but only because he was scared of chaos.

I was no longer going to be scared of chaos. I was going to be light and fun and adaptable. I was going to be bold and try new things and be my own person. The best way to do that was to make decisions my old self wouldn't make, so whatever Isaac frowned at, I would do, and whatever Ivy chose, I would choose.

I'd been one extreme for too long. If I tried something new for a little while, maybe I'd find a middle that fit.

"Hawk?" I asked, staring straight into Isaac's frown. "Could you get me a beer?"

All three of them stared at me.

"If you can't, that's fine."

"I can. They never card me, but—"

"But what? Won't I blend in better with a beer in my hand?"

"Eden," Billie clipped, short and crisp.

Isaac glanced at her. "You didn't tell me this was part of the deal."

Hawk raised an eyebrow and slid out of his seat. Yeah, I wouldn't want to be around for this conversation either.

"I didn't *know* this was part of the deal," she hissed at him. Then back to me, "Eden, what are you doing?"

"We're seniors, give me a break."

"One date with this delinquent and you're drinking?" Isaac asked.

"Two dates," I snapped back. One beer I hadn't even drunk yet, and this is what I got. "What's the big deal?"

"Bad choices make for bad people," he muttered.

"That's so myopic." Crossing my arms, I stared ahead as the band took the stage. They plugged themselves in, did some cute mic checks, joking with each other and the crowd, then got right to it.

The overall vibe was pretty great: the atmosphere sizzling due to the anticipation of a good show, the funky lights, and the decorative shelving behind the bar. Hawk clasped hands with the bartender, said a few words, and was walking back with two beers in no time.

Pulling out my phone, I bent sideways to capture the backlit shelf cubbies, then backwards for the industrial ceiling lights, and down for some feet near us—a pair of scrubby tennis shoes next to some glossy pink heels.

Then the first notes came out of Ivy's mouth. I'd seen her sing before, but here her performance made more sense. What seemed like trying too hard at a school concert freshman year felt electric in a bar with a band behind her. She lit the place up, like she'd found the pulse of the room, taken hold of it, and got it thumping through everyone's chest at once.

She could move, that was for sure. Every guy in the place was about drooling into his beer. I tore my focus from her to check on Hawk and his state of drooling, but found him watching me.

I smiled and took a sip of the beer he'd set on the table, trying hard not to cough and choke. Wow, that was disgusting.

Isaac leaned forward so we could hear him. "Twenty-eight people die every day from drunk driving accidents."

"Ah, but I'm not driving."

He cut a look over to Hawk, who lifted up his glass. "Ginger beer and lime."

"Exactly." Isaac looked smug, but Billie flicked him for being a jerk or an idiot—maybe both.

"Ginger beer, like root beer," Hawk explained. "It's non-alcoholic."

I was proud to say Hawk didn't look smug. He, for one, wasn't trying to rub anything in anyone's face.

A slower song came on. Not like a slow dance, but slow enough that it would be easier for two people to move together. "Do you still want to dance?" I asked. Because I was going to do all the new things. Also, Isaac was stifling me.

"Of course?" Hawk wrinkled his forehead in question.

"Yeah, I'm sorry about last night." What a downer I'd been. *No, I don't dance. No, I don't swim.* Except I do; I'm a swimmer. Or at least I had been.

Ugh. No more of that. I took another gulp of the piss-water people called a good time and stood up, offering a hand to him. He took it and we weaved through the tables to the little area that had been cleared for dancing.

I tried not to think, tried to just *do,* to let the beat move my whole body like the radio could get my foot tapping. We moved together, but apart, and I got whiffs of the ginger lime of his breath—fresh, fresher than mine probably after that beer, which is what the bar itself smelled like. Stale beer and body odor, plus multiple clouds of perfume warring for attention. It was the only part of the experience living up to the disdain my friends and I had previously held for such a scenario.

When the song crawled to a stop, Hawk asked, "Are Billie and Isaac together?"

"Like Wes and I were together, I guess." Loosely connected but with no formal boundaries.

He glanced back at them. "They look like they're together."

Isaac's head rested on Billie's. His free arm was thrown across her lap, which she held in both of her own. Turning back to the hazel of Hawk's eyes, I couldn't deny it. "Okay, so they are more than we were. But Billie is all about independence and power. She doesn't want to be held down by anything but herself."

"She thinks a boyfriend will hold her down?"

"Yep." And extreme opinions like that were what made Billie's one-woman show at the local theater worth watching—

her extreme opinions bolstered by brilliantly convincing arguments. If you heard her talk on feminism, for example, you wouldn't want to be held down either. Woman power all the way, no shackles.

"A shout out to my best friend!" Ivy screamed from the stage. We both turned. "Hawk Taylor, who writes our lyrics. I love you, Hawk!"

She pointed, and the whole world turned their attention to us. I would've stumbled back had he not been holding me in place.

Hawk raised his hand in acknowledgement, then skimmed it back around my waist and steered me off the makeshift dance floor.

"She knows better than to call me out like that," he grumbled as he sat back down. "She was just showing me off."

Or staking her claim. "She doesn't need to show you off," I said, settling in my seat. "You do a pretty good job of that yourself."

He let out a short, abrupt laugh. "I'm a show-off, huh?"

"That's not what I meant."

He leaned in and whispered, "I know that's not what you meant."

Turning toward him, I took an unsteady breath at how intimate it felt, how serious his face was set.

Isaac tapped me on the shoulder. "Check your texts."

"Whatever you have to say to me, just say it."

His gaze jumped to Hawk for a flat second, then to the table. He at least had the decency to mutter it: "It was supposed to be the four of us. You, me, Billie, and Wes."

And why was that? Just because we were the four swim team stars in middle school? What kind of crap was that to hang my first love on?

"If Wes wanted me that bad," I hissed, "he should've made it clear a long time ago."

"He was trying to not push you."

"Well, he hardly showed up."

"He's not a knight in effing armor, Eden."

"Of course not, there isn't really such a thing anymore, is there?"

"Because there shouldn't be," Billie piped up, from my other shoulder. "No woman needs a man to save her."

I twisted in my chair and glared at both of them. "I'm not asking to be saved. I just want a guy who treats me like a knight might."

Isaac leaned back in his seat. "Better make sure you're acting like a lady then, if you want to be treated like one."

Billie and I both turned on him, and my mouth dropped open, but Hawk beat us to it. "How she acts should have no influence on whether or not she's treated like a lady."

Isaac rolled his eyes, but Billie's shoulders dropped, clearly impressed.

I nodded in Hawk's direction. "Knight. Right there. Whether

you see it or not." Yes, I was leaning into the smug look on my face.

Putting a hand up before he could say any more, I fumed through the rest of the show while Hawk's arm rested behind me. When the set was over and the place clearing out, I stood and spun around. "I'll see you tomorrow." It was directed at Isaac, and it wasn't a request.

"I thought we were going to Ivy's," he said.

"We are. You aren't." I snatched my jacket off the back of the chair and headed toward the stage, where we were supposed to meet up with the band.

Scrambling to his feet, Isaac caught my arm. "I'm just looking out for you."

"Me or Wes?"

"Both. Both of you. How can I not?" He turned to Hawk. "You're a good guy, man. No hard feelings." Then back to me. "I'll be on my best behavior."

"Your best behavior isn't good enough."

Billie tugged on his shirt. "Come on. Let's go make out in your car."

"I wasn't trying to be a jerk, Eden," Isaac said.

"You don't have to try, Isaac. You just are sometimes."

He stared at me, and I stared right back. Billie pulled on his sleeve to get him moving, and after they'd turned, she mouthed a *sorry* over her shoulder.

I nodded. I knew.

This is how it was with us. With the four of us. With me and Isaac. He had a lecture in him for every situation, and he could never let anything go. One more reason to try out something new.

"Is he really a jerk?" Hawk asked, as we watched them go.

"His mouth gets the better of him once in a while."

"And you broke his best friend's heart last night."

"I guess."

He took my hand in his and pulled me toward the stage.

Ivy kissed Hawk on the cheek. "Thanks, baby. Couldn't do it without you."

"Anytime."

Yeah, that announcement was maybe laying claim.

"You were great, Ivy." I hoped my smile came off genuine enough, rather than sticky. Because what I wanted to say—though I'd never—was that Hawk was my date, so please keep your mouth to yourself.

She beamed at me. "Thanks. Glad you could make it. A friend of Hawk's is a friend of mine."

I opened my mouth to tell her we were more than friends, but the drummer came up and stuck his tongue down her throat, so I guess maybe it was okay to leave that unsaid. I slid slightly behind Hawk to avoid the very public display, and let him lead me outside.

Crisp autumn air cut through the stale remnants the bar had left in my nose. I held a deep breath, exhaling only once we were in Hawk's car.

As we pulled onto the street in his ancient orange bug, creaky and darkened with rust, we passed Isaac's shiny Lincoln Navigator. I laid on the horn and waved as they came up for air.

Hawk laughed. "I didn't think she was serious."

"Oh, she's always serious."

"So when she told me she'd twist corkscrews into my eyeballs if I wasn't a gentleman from start to finish, she meant it?"

"She did not say that." I covered my face with my hands and groaned. "She would totally say something like that."

"Personally, I was impressed with her ingenuity."

Leaning my shoulder against the seat, I smiled. "Don't worry, you could totally take her."

He tightened his grip on the wheel. "You think that's who I am?"

"What? No. It's just something people say."

He glanced over at me, like he didn't buy it.

"I mean, sure, you seem like you could hold your own." He *was* carved with ocean salt and harsh storms. There were so many contradictions beneath his surface already, deep valleys I wanted to discover. There was nothing wrong with that; it's just who he was. And it was a nice change from Wes's refinement.

He pulled into an apartment complex and parked the car, turned it off, and gazed out his window. "Know why the teachers let me be late and don't kick me out?"

"I guess I never thought about it."

"My brother kicked the shit out of Mr. Greavy. That's why he got expelled, along with some other stuff."

Thankfully, he wasn't looking at me, because I could feel my face doing all sorts of surprised contorting.

"He's seven years older than me, so only the adults remember him. And they figure, as long as I'm doing the work and getting decent grades, well, it's far more than they would've expected from Hank." He squinted over at me, or maybe it was a wince.

His hair was long enough it was starting to curl at the ends, and he had a cut on his chin I hadn't noticed before. He must have shaved for me again.

"When no one expects anything of you," he said. "You start to expect nothing of yourself."

"You can't give up on yourself like that. Or your brother. People change."

"My dad has never changed."

"What do you mean?"

"I mean he's always been shitty to people, and he still says the same shitty things. He still gets off on picking fights, even though he's forty, and he can't keep a job."

"Fine. But if he wanted to change, he could. He just needs to decide to." I knew because I was deciding to right now. "What would you want to do with your life, if you knew anything was possible?"

"You don't ask easy questions, huh?" But his lip twitched and he finally turned to me. Really turned to me. No glancing and dancing back, but a complete attention and focus. It was something I was really starting to like.

I grinned. "Answer it or distract me, those are your options."

He took his time putting his hands to my face and brushed one thumb along my cheek before placing his lips on mine. We started at determined this time and heated up from there, to a place I'd never fallen into before, a place I hadn't known kisses could go.

He ran his fingers down my collarbone, thumbs sliding across my shoulders, pulling the neck of my shirt wider and exposing my skin. He leaned down to kiss me on the outside curve of my shoulder, but before he landed, he stopped himself.

From one kiss in three months to shoulder kisses on day three. Maybe Isaac was right. Maybe Hawk was like that, or at the very least used to that. Maybe I didn't know what I was getting myself into.

Hawk released me to grip the steering wheel and exhaled a windstorm, while I twisted my watch around my wrist.

Screw you, Isaac. It was just a shoulder. The spot ached now, the skin reaching out to know what his lips would have felt like there.

"I didn't ask you to stop," I said.

"I'm not who Isaac thinks I am. What he's trying to protect you from."

"Isaac would be protecting me from anyone except Wes. You get that, right? It has nothing to do with you."

"But I'm trying to figure out what else a girl like you would want from a guy like me."

I flapped my mouth open and closed a few times. That sounded like self-doubt, like he was as uncertain about what I'd see in him as I was about what he'd see in me. And I knew there was no way around it—it was my turn now, to take his hand in mine. "It's not about what I want from you; it's just that I do want you. I don't know why, or what for, and I don't care. I just know I do."

His gaze held mine for a moment. "I will be your knight in shining armor, Eden. I can be that."

"I'm not looking for someone to save me."

"But you want someone to feel safe with."

Our eyes locked. He'd heard me. Billie thought I was naive and Isaac thought it was a joke. Wes had been too lazy, but Hawk had heard me.

It wasn't that he was this different, intriguing species I was enthralled with. That's all I'd seen, but maybe that wasn't the point. The point was he got me. He was the right fit.

10

Inside the apartment, Ivy was still the star of the show.

It was her, her cousin Jay, Hawk, me, and Suckface Drummer Boy, which got me wondering if it was normally just her and three guys.

Jay played guitar, and the guy who'd played bass had gone home with a groupie, as best I could tell. Hawk wrote their lyrics, I now knew, so maybe this was who he spent his time with—maybe the band spent all their time together.

Ivy was orchestrating a game of Spades in Jay's small kitchen/living room. He was definitely older than us, college-age maybe, though I'm not sure he was actually in school. Ivy apparently spent a lot of time there, as she'd been the one to set out snacks and drinks on the counter, had slipped into a bedroom to change into yoga pants and an oversized t-shirt, had fished a deck of cards out of the sofa like she knew exactly where she'd left them, and had curled up at the table, feet on the seat and knees to her chin.

"Eden, baby, come play with us," she said.

Okay, so she called everyone baby. Good to know.

The small kitchen table fit only four chairs, and Hawk sat down in the last open seat. I sidled up next to him and leaned against the wood.

"Do you know how to play?" he asked.

I shook my head. Uno was as far as I'd gotten with cards.

He pushed back from the table and patted his lap. I scanned the room, but there was nothing else to sit on—no ottoman, no little table, not even a laundry basket or crate. And I wasn't about to ask if they had a folding chair hiding somewhere. Certainly Ivy wouldn't think twice about sitting on a guy's lap, so I wasn't going to either.

As gracefully as I could, I slid on. Hawk put his arms up on either side of me to hold the cards Ivy was dealing out.

I tried to relax. Though we'd melted into each other on the dance floor, this seemed like something else—a casual type of comfort that came only after much more getting to know one another.

Ivy was explaining the rules for my sake, but Hawk's presence behind me—his chest against my back, his arms loosely brushing mine, his breath dancing across my cheek—was so distracting I only heard half her words.

They went around the table to bid for who wanted trump, whatever that meant. Hawk won and picked—"call" was the term he used—but after the hand had been played, he lost points.

Cries went up around the table:

"What's wrong with you, man?"

"Yeah, dude, where's your head at?"

"You play," he whispered, as Suckface dealt again.

"I don't know how." I turned a little but that only ratcheted up the intensity, what with his nose nearly on my cheek, so I looked forward again, and quick.

"Lose, I don't care." He set the cards on the table. "I can't focus with you in my lap."

I moved to get up but he caught my waist with one arm. "I can sit somewhere else, Hawk. I could stand." I brushed my hair over one shoulder and tried to look at him without our faces touching.

"I don't want you to. Unless you'd be more comfortable somewhere else?"

No. Or, well, I didn't want to move. I shook my head and realized everyone was watching us.

"The makings of a new song," Jay said. He had the same orbed eyes and washed out complexion as Ivy, but his hair was a golden brown and his irises warmed with honey.

"How is losing at cards a new song?" Suckface asked.

"With you in my lap..." Ivy sang. *"...I can't focus on my...my..."*

"My rap!" Jay cried, a finger in the air.

Snickers sounded all around but I shifted uncomfortably, only to freeze up when I realized I was shifting on Hawk's lap, which was currently the subject of conversation.

"I can see why you write the lyrics," I muttered to Hawk.

"That's not really the kind of stuff I write," he said.

"You don't need to tell us that," Jay said.

"No, but he needs to make sure Eden knows." Ivy looked at

me. "Of all of us, Hawk's the least like that. I should know. I've tried and tried to get him to sleep with me, but he's all, 'can't mix friendship and sex. Can't mix business and sex'. I say, what about mixing friendship and business, you don't seem to have a problem with that."

"Don't listen to her," Hawk whispered. "She's never tried to sleep with me."

"If she had, I'd a punched him out," Suckface said, leaning toward Ivy while making a kissy face.

She giggled and shoved him away.

"She's sort of like Isaac," Hawk explained. "You can't take her word too much to heart."

The slight difference being she totally made stuff up while Isaac was as honest as they came, but I let it slide.

"My word *is* my heart," Ivy said, pointing at her chest. "Better to be all of what you are, than half of what everyone else wants you to be."

I held up my water. "Cheers to that."

She grinned at me, lifting up her beer.

I got another crash course in Spades. Ivy was my partner, and she pretty much carried me, but I didn't make any stupid mistakes, thanks to Hawk whispering in my ear before I might have. I was better for the second game and had it down by the middle of the third.

"She's a shark!" Jay cried, with an appreciative grin.

"I got bit by a shark once," Ivy said, lifting her right hand in the air to show off a nasty scar on her elbow. Then she tucked her feet under her and leaned forward over the table, a bulbous locket sliding out from under her t-shirt and swaying in front of her chest, as if everything about her was working to hypnotize me. Even her voice changed, going softer and more melodic.

"My mom was dating this surfer when she lived in Hawaii. I was ten, only there for a week, so he brought us to his favorite place—totally secluded, dripping with trees, green and blue as far as the eye could see. I'd never been in the ocean before, never seen a reef, nothing, so he went big. My mom's boyfriends always went big. Anyway, I'm out on the board, the waves pulling me farther and farther out, while I'm trying to stand up, or even kneel on the stupid thing, when my mom starts yelling that I need to come back. So I turned myself around and paddled back on my belly. I was maybe ten feet from them when it got me. The pain wiped everything out—the green, the blue—it was all blinding sun. It felt like the sun. Burning, a million degrees."

She straightened up, set her chin on her hand and her mangled elbow to the table. "I passed out and when I woke up I was at the hospital, elbow all stitched up and a huge shark stuffed animal snuggled against me. My mom was always big about getting back on the horse, facing your fears; I guess that stuffed shark was her way to get me back on. Not that I've ever been in the ocean since."

She shrugged, gathered the deck, and started shuffling. The cards whooshed and swooshed at a dizzying rate, as if she were chasing something away. I wasn't sure I believed her story, but she was definitely mesmerizing.

I wanted that. I wanted to be mesmerizing and contagious. More Ivy. Less Isaac. I only needed to find the secret to infusing a little of her inside of me.

~

The ride home was quiet. No radio, no conversation. Only Hawk's thumb rubbing back and forth on my skin.

When he pulled up in front of my house, he broke the silence. "I can't see you tomorrow."

I looked over, the streetlight slanting in across his shoulder.

"I'm supposed to be with my dad."

"I have plans and homework and stuff anyway." All true, not that I wouldn't have skipped it if he'd asked me to. I unbuckled my seatbelt. Last night I'd been a bumbling bundle of nerves getting out of his car—even misinterpreting a goodnight kiss for a hug—and he'd smirked at me the whole way. Tonight, I was determined to be cool.

Except, I didn't really know what cool was. Maybe a quick kiss? I wasn't going to make out with him in case my mom could see us, but if I took off without anything, it might seem like I was upset that he didn't have time for me tomorrow.

We went for each other at the same time, too quickly, and bumped heads. I groaned, and he snickered a little. The way he never got ruffled should have been infuriating, but I loved that about him. I loved that he was chill no matter what, and I loved the way his face lit up in amusement so much of the time. From brooding poet to bare and open.

He reached out for my chin, pulling me forward slowly as he rested his forehead on mine, then tilting his face down so our cheeks brushed against each other before our lips met.

Three. Simple. Kisses.

When he released me, I had to bite my lip to keep from grinning like I'd won something. As I got out of the car, as I walked across the lawn, as I turned back to wave, as I entered the house and locked up behind me.

"Two nights out of three, huh?" My mom was leaning against the archway to the kitchen, a book and mug of tea on the table behind her. "When do I get to meet him?"

I shrugged. "When do I get to meet your new guy?"

She snorted a little and turned back her tea. "Touché, my love. Touché."

Sunday

First thing Sunday morning, I changed into my new bikini and stared at my reflection in the bathroom mirror for almost half an hour.

Every minute that ticked by I grew more certain I could wear it in the dark with Hawk. Still, I wasn't so sure I could wear it in the light of day with Billie, Wes, and Isaac. Billie wouldn't say anything. We'd already argued, she'd already acquiesced. The boys, however—Isaac was never able to keep his mouth shut, would probably steal words from Billie's stage essays and throw them at me, and Wes, well, I didn't want to encourage him.

But what if Hawk never took me swimming again and I didn't get a chance to wear it until next summer? By then, the magic could fade.

I loved this suit. I could hardly believe it, but I did. I loved the feeling it gave me, like I could conquer the world.

I wasn't the old Eden anymore—in fact, I was staring proof of that in the face. The new Eden took over last night and the worst that had happened was I'd fought with Isaac, which wasn't so hard to do in the first place.

With a nod, I threw a pair of shorts and tank over my new suit, then tied my hair up in a pony. On my way to the kitchen for a banana, I paused at the height marks my mom had made on our door frame over the years.

I could have grown a few inches, stretched out a bit and elongated. Only, as I stood against the marks, hand at the top of my head, my finger slid against the top notch in the wood. I'd need a scale to tell me if I'd actually lost weight, and if I hadn't, then what? The magic wasn't real? I didn't believe in aliens or plastic surgeon fairies, but I also didn't want to step on proof that nothing had actually changed, lest my mind, which I was starting to wonder about, crash back into reality.

The doorbell dinged. My mom was at the grocery store and Reese was practicing piano, his fingers slowly chopping their way across the old upright Grandpa had found at a junk shop and cleaned up for us.

I strode across the room, spotting Wes's car through the front window. Checking my watch as I opened the door, I verified he was three hours early.

"We study on Sundays," he explained.

This was true. And seeing as I'd pretty much forgotten about school since Wednesday when I woke up perfect, I could use some studying.

"I figured if I waited until after our swim, you might... Well, I thought you might have plans tonight." He held up a coffee for me, and I realized he'd never before had to think about who else I might be with, or what I might be doing that would conflict with him. Because if I wasn't with him, I was with Billie, and he knew he was welcome anytime.

Taking the plain, ink-free, disposable coffee cup with a thank-you smile, I headed for the kitchen table, letting him close the door and follow me.

I took a sip and then another. "What is this?" He knew what I drank at every shop across town and this wasn't any of them.

"What does it taste like?"

I tried it again, rolling the coffee around on my tongue a bit before swallowing. "Both of my favorite fall flavors."

His face lit up. "You seem a little sick of the same old, same old, so I thought I'd change it up a bit."

I slid into my chair. "It's not bad, together."

"No, we certainly aren't."

Raising my eyebrows, I replied, "This is supposed to be you and me in here?"

He slid into his seat and rummaged in his bag. "I'm the sweet, you're the salty."

With a short, hopefully not encouraging laugh, I threw a pencil at him. He caught it and twirled it into place. "Calculus first, then?" I asked.

"Or psych."

"Calc," I decided. I might have planned to do that psych project on myself, but I wasn't ready to face it.

"Remember when we used to put off math until last?" he asked.

"I remember when *you* used to put off math until last."

"Then you explained basic arithmetic with a story problem about us—what was it? If you came over to my house for three hours every Saturday, and I came over to yours for five hours every Sunday, and this lasted for seven years, the numerical strength of our relationship would be x by the time we hit college?" He looked down. "After that I always wanted to start with it, hoping we could somehow keep increasing x."

I cocked my head at him, but the pencil in his hand was innocently working its way across his paper. So, he was saying math reminded him of me. And I reminded him of math.

Just one more reason I needed a change. We managed to work in silence for four minutes before Reese army-crawled in and made a fort under the table.

Good, then at least Wes wouldn't bring up Hawk.

Three minutes later, he asked, "The predatory bird is treating you okay?"

Or he'd just speak in code. "Really? The predatory bird?"

"Would you prefer dirty bird?" He was keeping a pretty good poker face.

"How about I throw a pen at you?"

Glancing up, he countered, "How about you remember who brought you your favorite coffee in the whole world?"

I pushed my lips out a little bit. "The bird brought me coffee the other morning."

"Did he now?" Wes pushed back from the table, the chair tilting off its feet. "Was it your favorite?"

I didn't answer. It had not been my favorite, but there was no way Hawk could have known that. He'd seen the outside of the cup a million times, sure, but never the inside. Wes, on the other hand, had been around long enough to have knowledge of the actual contents.

Reese poked his head up next to Wes. "Are you guys talking about the middle finger?" He sprung it up from his fist, and Wes smothered it with his hand.

"Dude, don't let your mom see that. It's disrespectful." Wes let go of him and set his chair back to normal. "Now, get back to work, you're losing ground down there."

Wes watched me while my brother disappeared back under the table. "You didn't answer my question."

"You think I'd put up with someone not treating me well?"

"Must I remind you of Jacob?"

"Hey, Jacob treated all three of us like princesses. Anyway, everyone wanted a piece of that. I should've been happy there weren't ten of us."

Wes laughed. "If only he was still a practicing polygamist. That was quality entertainment."

"Seriously. What twelve-year-old claims Mormonism, just to make the rest of us okay with his cheating?"

His face went serious. "I was never okay with him doing that to you."

A moment passed. Reese's army tank noises filled the space between us, and I wondered if this was what I would have to endure now—constant assaults on the history we shared, sudden reveals of how he'd felt then, and the hidden implication that he made more sense for me.

But that was the problem. I didn't want to make *sense* with someone. I wanted things to feel senseless—to be so swept up it might feel irrational, yet inevitable and unavoidable too.

Wes leaned over, hands on the table and elbows up behind him. "You didn't give me enough time," he whispered. "I haven't had enough time."

"You had three months, not to mention all the years before that."

He leaned back in his chair, watching me for a minute watching him. "I thought we had something. I know you wouldn't have done all this on purpose, but it feels like... I thought we were... I thought you liked me."

"I did, Wes—I do—but I like Hawk." More, I wanted to say. I liked him more. After running my hands over my face, I said it, so there was no doubt: "I'm with him right now. It happened and that's where we're at, okay?"

His eyes took the hit, clouding over like I'd rained on his

birthday cake, but, like the gentleman he was, he picked up his pencil and got back to work.

"Hey, Wes?" I asked, a moment later.

"Yeah?" But he kept his gaze down.

"Do you think I look any different?"

He rolled his eyes up to me. "You mean, do you have the rosy glow of love about you?"

"No!" Did he really think I'd rub it in his face like that? "No, I mean, do you think my hair looks different, or my shoulders, my eyes, my lips…" I trailed off because his gaze hit each of these places as I said them, and maybe bringing up my lips *was* rubbing his face in it. I looked down at the formulas on my paper and wished I could take it all back. "Never mind."

I willed it to go away—all of it—the conversation, my need for confirmation, my need to be seen.

"You look great, as always," he finally said. "And maybe you have a confident glow about you, since Hawk. Confidence, not love. You can't possibly be in love yet. Please don't be in love."

He was holding his pencil tight, forcing his fingertips red, but as I looked up, he looked down. Just like the past six months, he went shy when I was interested, and I went timid when he was ready. Taking turns backing off from each other hadn't gotten us anywhere.

Or, I guess, it had gotten us here.

"It's only been a few days," I said. "Of course I'm not in love yet."

"Isaac said you looked serious."

Reese's bomb explosion noises peppered a gaping hole in our conversation. After a particularly terrible sounding battle, during which many people died (I knew this because of the "Man down! Man down! Where are our reinforcements?"), Wes asked, "So, *are* you serious?"

It felt serious. Hawk seemed serious. I wanted it to be serious. But I didn't want to admit it yet. It was too soon. I didn't want to jinx it, didn't want to sound silly, and didn't want to hurt Wes. If only I knew how to tell him the truth without doing all of those things. He was one of my oldest friends. A best.

I finally went with: "If that's what Isaac says."

"Isaac only said it looked that way." He nudged my knee with his foot, under the table, and our eyes finally met. "But you can't judge a book by its movie."

We'd heard that somewhere and ran away with it. But he couldn't pick and choose where to apply it: "Then maybe you shouldn't judge Hawk by his movie."

Wes frowned.

I did my best at imitating my brother's bomb noise, complete with hand motions, then finished in a golf announcer's voice, "She says for the win."

He shook his head, and as I took a sip of my new favorite coffee, he slipped under the table to go to war with my brother.

~

Wes drove me to Isaac's for our final swim, where everything felt comfortable, familiar, and old. Like nothing had changed, not even me—at least, until we stripped down to our suits and they saw my bikini.

Wes blinked, many times, and Isaac raised an eyebrow. Billie smirked and pushed me in. I straightened my arms and set my body rigid so I'd sink faster, until my toes, then heels, hit the bottom. Complete silence, suspension, an alternate universe. Maybe that was it; maybe I'd woken up in an alternate universe. Only, more would be different if that were true. Pushing off the base of the pool, I opened my eyes and watched the bubbles as I exhaled and shot back up to the surface. There was just something about being in the water.

"Who's gonna race me?" I asked, when I emerged. Wes was still standing there, dumbfounded, looking at me as if I'd sprouted a horn.

"Sure you won't lose your bottoms?" Isaac asked.

Billie smacked him. "Don't be such an idiot." Then she pulled off her oversized tee to reveal the bikini her mom must have bought her. Solidarity. And diversion. Now they were staring at her.

Treading water, I grinned. "What, because I'm so fast?"

"Not as fast as me," Billie said, diving in for a head start. I caught up to her feet, and reached for one, almost had it, but she shot away from me. She did a legit flip turn when she reached the edge, but I didn't go all the way to the wall, so I could catch up a bit. Which meant when I beat her, she cried cheater.

"Pumpkin eater!" she yelled, spitting water at me. But we were both laughing.

"Are you guys coming in or what?" I asked. "Who's going to race the winner?" I raised a hand. "Me, I'm the winner."

"Cheater!" Billie cried.

Wes could barely look at me. Granted, there was a lot more cleavage happening than normal. But honestly.

"Wes, race me."

"Yeah?"

"Yeah."

He nodded. "No cheating, though." And he held a hand out to help me up, so we could dive off together at the same time.

Isaac slid into the pool at the corner, the judge's spot, so he could call it if it was close, but we all knew Wes was going to kill me. He and Isaac were just too fast, and I didn't do this regularly anymore.

He shot ahead so quickly I couldn't have grabbed for anything, then shot past me again, like a blink.

I leisurely made my way back and shoved him. "Good job."

Normally, he would've shoved me back, with maybe a "You can do better," but today there was no touching, just a soft glance, and a "You too."

Maybe what Hawk had done was open a can of worms that neither Wes nor I had been ready to open. We hadn't been ready for change, but Hawk had forced it, forced Wes to tell me how he felt, forced me to see this bikini through his eyes.

I did not, however, feel comfortable enough in my new suit to just wrap a towel around my waist when Isaac's mom told us that the food was ready. Instead, I threw my shorts and tank back on, even though they'd get wet. Truth be told, I'd always been intimidated by Isaac's mom. She was dainty, artfully dressed, hair sleek and shiny, makeup so perfect and natural she looked like she didn't have any makeup on at all. Full of genuine smiles, she oozed a kind of no-nonsense confidence while still managing to be welcoming.

Their house was huge, grand in many ways, but decorated comfortably so you forgot how big it was if you spent enough time there. The spread in the kitchen was straight from Pinterest and geared for a seven-year-old's swim party. It was why Isaac never invited anyone but us over. I nibbled on "drift wood" and "crab legs" in "seaweed dip" (pretzels and carrots in spinach artichoke dip) while Billie and Isaac's mom caught up. They were strange together, avid and excitable, especially when they got talking politics. Isaac stood nearby, interrupting every sentence or two.

Billie was wearing the same black shorts that I was, and a t-shirt that read *Talk nerdy to me*. My tank had a bee sketched out on it, but was nearly the same heather gray, and our hair hung in similar wet kinks down our backs. Hers was more red than mine when dry, and her freckles darker, but suddenly I could see it, how similar we really were. She had smaller breasts and narrower hips, but we were both five foot six.

When Hawk had said "same difference," he hadn't meant it to be insulting. It was probably how the entire school saw us. I couldn't deny that we'd grown so close as to be nearly indistinguishable. Same interests, same grades, same friends, same life. The only difference was my volleyball versus her open mic.

"It's been so long since the four of you came for lunch," Isaac's mom was saying, looking around at us. "You should come tomorrow. I'm sure we'll have leftovers, and I could make those beef and cheese pockets you like."

"That sounds great, Mrs. Anderson," Billie said, glancing over to me.

She caught my eye and grabbed for my hand. "It's so nice to see you, Eden."

I nodded. "You too, Mrs. Anderson."

Letting go, she checked with Wes. "Monday, then?"

"Monday," he agreed, shooting a look over to me. I nodded.

~

After Wes dropped me at home, I spent a lot of time studying the pattern of the bleachers. At the side of the house, from my bedroom's window seat, I could see the football field across the street and the school partially concealed by the stands.

It seemed ridiculous, how confident I'd felt simply wearing a stupid bikini one day of my life. Sure, I could hide behind Billie's ideals, but really, I'd been afraid of walking outside the square she'd boxed us into.

Closing my eyes, I hoped to remember this the next time something came up that I wouldn't normally have done, something Isaac would blanch at and that would raise an eyebrow from Wes. It was power, doing things that scared you. That's what I'd realized today. And that's what I saw in Ivy— that same kind of power—seeing something you wanted, even if it might scare you a little, and taking it by the throat.

A noise made me jump, and I opened my eyes to see Hawk standing at the window in front of me. I blinked a few times, not sure if seeing things was the second step to going crazy.

He mimed opening the window, and I pushed up the pane.

"Hey," I whispered, glad I hadn't been bugging my mom about replacing the screen. The top and right side were unattached, and the mesh was folded over like an envelope flap. "How's your dad?"

"Mean."

"I'm sorry."

"At least I can count on him for something. Do you mind?" His finger was at the top left corner, threatening the screen with total annihilation.

I shook my head and he ripped it the rest of the way down, then tore it off. I grabbed it from him and tucked it under my seat, then kneeled on the floor so we were eye level.

Leaning, in, he propped his arms on the cushion, then set his chin on them. "What'd you do today?"

"Studied…"—it got caught in my throat but I forced it out—"…with Wes. Then swam at Isaac's." I worried about his expression, but it didn't seem to change much. "Do you want to come in? Should I come out?"

"No, I just came to say good night." He motioned for me to come closer, then leaned in as far as he could to meet me for a kiss. It brought back everything from the weekend, pre-today—the diner and the bay, the bar and Ivy, the person I was now going to be.

"Did Ivy really get bit by a shark?" I asked.

He pulled back and considered the question. "It's hard to tell. Sometimes she tells it like it is, and sometimes she's performing."

"Doesn't that bother you?"

He shrugged. "Not really."

The wind whistled past us into my room, and our watches ticked to the pattern of my thoughts. Honestly, no matter how much I wanted to or tried, I would never be like her. Not all the way. She lived with abandon, and I cared too much. If that's what he wanted, it wouldn't take long for him to realize how not like her I was.

"Did Wes try to kiss you again?" he asked.

I shook my head.

"I like you, Eden. I thought about you all day, about how we've barely spent any time together, but how I don't want you kissing anyone else. That's why I'm here." He drummed his fingers along his arm. "Is it too soon to ask for that?"

As if I went around kissing everyone all the time. As if I even had more than two lip possibilities in my life. "Not too soon," I whispered, and his forehead uncreased. "But I am going to be on time for school tomorrow."

"Of course you are," he replied, with a soft half grin. Hopping up a little, he gave me a final last kiss and a bigger smile, before turning to cross our side lawn. I waited until I couldn't see him anymore before closing the window and climbing back up on the seat.

Things were changing, I could feel it. I was changing. Because of him or because of the new me, I didn't know, and I wasn't sure it mattered.

Change wasn't something I'd ever really searched out, especially after we left my dad. Billie and I had been new friends back when all that went down, but close already, and maybe I'd clung to her, to everything that was familiar, in order to remember what it was like back when he'd been there.

Plus, Billie was as stable as they came, even though I'd been the strong one when we'd first come together in third grade. Jonathon had pushed her off a huge snow bank and she'd slid down, somehow managing a cut by her eye, to land at my feet. Looking up at me, the fiercest and surest girl in our class, I could see the wobble of her lip and the fat tear in her eye. The look on her face was severe though, as if by mentioning it, I'd betray her, as if there would be no speaking of the fact that she had ever been, or ever would be, weak.

Already in third grade.

I'd stepped back, rather than offering her a hand, and said "I scraped my knee and need a band-aid. Will you come to the nurse's office with me?"

Her fat tear receded, and the wobble in her lip was forced clear with a smile. She held out her hand and I took it, helped her up, and spent ten minutes arguing with the nurse that I did indeed have a very small and painful cut on my knee that she couldn't see. Ten minutes of Billie getting cleaned, sanitized, and bandaged up. Ten minutes of solidifying us as a unit.

I'd only been strong for her that day because she needed it. She hadn't since, so I'd let her take the lead. I always depended on her strength, and my mom's, but now I wanted some for myself. And something about Hawk had me feeling like he was the key to finding it.

My strength had to be apart from them, and he existed where my friends dared not go.

Monday

Waking up that next morning was a little easier, trusting that I would still look like the new me. But man, did I want a cheeseburger, a juicy one with ketchup and cheese dripping off the sides.

My stomach groaned at the thought, and I hurried up for the sake of breakfast. My mom had made scrambled eggs with feta, onions and mushrooms—plus green peppers for her, minus onions for my brother.

I ruffled his hair and sank down into my chair. There was nothing wrong with a cheeseburger once in a while, so I'd ask Hawk to take me. See if he had anything to say about a girl ordering a double at the drive thru.

Pulling out my phone, I texted him under the eagle eyes of my mother. I had about five seconds before she'd snatch it away.

Send, pocket, and back to shoveling food. His response

buzzed, but I didn't check it. My mom was on to discussing the day's schedule.

"I want you home by five tonight, Eden." She took two quick bites of eggs, then two quicker sips of coffee. "We'll be having a guest for dinner."

My brother sat up straighter and I can't say I didn't too. "A guest?"

She put her fork down and tucked her hands in her lap.

I gasped. She let out a little smile.

"What?" Reese asked, looking back and forth between us. "What kind of guest?"

Her face went soft and she smiled gently at my brother. "I've been having lunch at work with someone for a while now. I'd like to bring him home to meet you. Is that okay?"

Reese's forehead curled. "It sounds like he's already coming."

My mom reached out to squeeze his hand. "He'll be here at 5:30, and I want you both home in time to set the table and clean your rooms. Okay?" She loosened her grip and went back to her eggs. "You'll like him, I'm sure of it."

With my pocket buzzing again, I shoveled down the rest of my breakfast and drained my orange juice. Mondays were my one free night, no volleyball. I didn't usually spend it at home. But this was the first guy she'd mentioned in maybe five years.

I wasn't silly enough to think she hadn't seen anyone else since then, but after the last one was exiled, Reese had asked about him for months, and then again on Christmas the next year.

If my mom was bringing a guy home, she must really be serious.

~

"I'll have a hamburger meal, please. No cheese."

"I'll have a double cheeseburger, no meal, and you can throw his cheese on mine."

At the window, Hawk rifled through his wallet for a ten. I pulled a five out of my pocket and held it out to him, but he ignored it.

I tucked the money in his middle console as he passed the bag over, and he drove back to school, the scent of greasy fast food edging out the faint smell of oil I'd come to associate with his ancient Bug.

He pulled the bag off my lap and reached inside, then handed me my cheeseburger, which I'd been nearly shaking with anticipation for.

"I can hardly fit this in my mouth," I muttered, trying it from a few angles.

Drawing his eyebrows together slightly, he took it from me, squished it between his hands, and handed it back. "Now try."

No wink, no condescending smile. Only here, let me help you. It worked too, and made the ketchup drip down the sides like I'd imagined it.

As we ate, he searched for a radio station.

"Do you think I've looked different lately?" I asked, once he seemed satisfied with the music. "I mean, maybe you didn't notice me before, but—"

"I've always noticed you." He said it flippantly, between a swallow and a bite.

"You have?"

"Your walk is hard not to notice."

"My walk?"

"You have a very confident walk. I always wondered how you could walk around like you owned the place and then hide behind your friends the way you do."

I mulled over his words for a second but wanted an answer first. "I look the same to you that I always have?"

"Yes."

"One hundred percent?"

"Yes, why? Do you feel different?"

"No! I mean, yes." I bit the inside of my lip. "Yes, I guess I do feel different."

"It doesn't matter how you look, Eden. It matters how you feel."

I slumped back in the seat, burger in my lap. "What do you mean hide behind my friends?"

"You always slide behind Billie or Wes or Isaac when they're talking to someone. I mean, you talk too, but it's like you need a shield." He offered me a fry. I shook my head and he popped it in his mouth. "And you were never alone. If you had been, I'd have talked to you earlier, intrigued by the shy girl with the confident walk."

"Not because of how I look?"

"What?"

"You were intrigued by how I walk, but not how I look?"

"How a person looks is not all that intriguing. It is what it is."

I took an extra big bite of my burger, and chewed on this. If I looked different only to myself, then I was seriously going crazy. And why did it irk me a little that he didn't seem to care how I looked? I mean, sure, I wanted him to like me for more than that, and Billie would positively kill me if she knew what I was thinking, but most importantly I wanted him to *see* me. To appreciate all the little things I was suddenly able to appreciate myself.

I threw the burger down on my lap, somewhat disgusted with my crippling insecurity, with the fact that no one else seemed to see me any differently, and that I couldn't get it all out of my head. Plus, it turns out a double burger is too high on the meat ratio. Not enough cheese, ketchup, and bun to even it out.

"Did I say something wrong?" Hawk asked.

"No."

"You sure?" He tapped a fry against its container.

I looked down at the rest of my burger. He'd finished his, but I'd only gotten three-fourths of the way through mine. And now my stomach was a little shaky. From the hunk of meat lodged in there or the boy sitting next to me, I wasn't sure. Regardless, I couldn't eat another bite. I folded the paper around it and dropped it in the bag.

When I looked back over to him, his face was serious. "Is this for real, Eden?" he asked. "Are you for real?"

"It is," I replied. "I am."

He leaned in slowly, eyes open until the moment before his lips were on mine, as if making sure I was up for this, making sure I wasn't wincing or pulling away. I rested into it and let him lead me slow and sultry like the classic music wafting out of the one speaker that still worked.

As the music crescendoed, so did we—fries tumbled to the floor, his hands found my knees, my palms landed on his arms, pulling him closer, inadvertently leading him to my thighs, then my waist. Thumbs sliding, catching skin. The heat of his touch on my hip bone seared into me for the tiniest pause, before he pulled back to find my hands, to anchor his fingers to mine. Holding them tight, he kissed me tighter.

His phone buzzed in the cup holder between us. We both looked down at it.

"Ivy wants you to hang out with her after school," he said, as her name lit up the screen.

"She does?"

Leaning back against the driver's side door, he ran a hand over his face and into his hair. "She's been bugging me all day."

"I'd rather just hang out with you."

His phone kept squirming, but he ignored it. "I'd rather hang out with you, too, but when Ivy gets something in her head, there's really no getting around it."

As the buzzing proved. "She can have me till five." I handed him his phone. "Now tell her to knock it off and leave us alone."

He texted her back, threw his cell in the back seat, and leaned forward for me. I diverted my face to his neck, taking a moment to breathe him in—clean soap, fresh laundry, and dusty vintage coat—before coming back for his lips.

Three languid moments were all we had before the back door swung open. Ivy slid her skinny butt across the seat, rested her pin-pointy elbows near each of our shoulders, and pushed her face between ours.

"I got some killer magazines yesterday." She pulled back a bit, like she might have realized what she'd interrupted and be bowing out gracefully. "You do like magazines, right? Jay and Hawk and Tony snore at me if I try to force fashion on them, but you're a girl, right?"

"She is a girl," Hawk said.

"I'm cool with magazines," I said, turning to her. "Who's Tony?"

"My boy-man. Also, party at my place this weekend."

I squinted at Hawk for explanation and he clarified, "The

drummer."

Ah, Suckface. Perhaps I'd had an unnatural obsession with suction and lips lately.

There was a tapping on my window—Wes, Isaac, and Billie—and it was then I remembered we'd planned just yesterday to go to Isaac's house for lunch.

Oops.

None of them glanced at me; just a knuckle tap and they were on their way. But they couldn't be mad about a silly lunch. Now that I had a boyfriend, they should expect me to miss a lunch here and there.

Yeah, probably just in a hurry to get to fifth period.

Then Ivy was talking my ear off about high-fashion magazines and why they were better than Pinterest, because of the glossy pages, or sometimes matte, and you couldn't print something off the computer and have it look as good on the walls, plus there was such an impact to tactile things, didn't I think?

But honestly, when it came to Ivy, she moved so fast, she didn't give me much time to think at all.

With her, your choices were to be swept up or get out of the way.

~

Ivy and I walked back to her cousin Jay's apartment after

school, which looked a lot shadier in the daylight. The parking lot was strewn with litter and small chunks of loose blacktop, while the grass had been left to die. No bushes lined the foundation, or even the entryway, and the rusty door made an awful groaning sound as she pulled it open. Inside, the hallway carpet was so worn it had gone bare in some places.

I followed Ivy up the stairs without touching the railing. It smelled amazing, though, like someone on the first floor was making garlic bread.

"I know it's not much," she said, unlocking the door as I studied a stain on the wall. "But the tradeoff is no one telling you what to do or how to think."

"You live here?" I asked, as she led me to the kitchenette without locking the door behind her. "I mean, on your own, with Jay?"

"Yep, for about two years now." She tossed her faux-leather jacket on the chair and rummaged for a bag of chips and two sodas.

"You've lived on your own since you were sixteen?"

"Twelve," she corrected, as I followed her into her room. "I moved into Jay's basement when I was twelve. Jay's dad was more like an uncle, though, even to him. His only rule was no staying out all night."

Twelve was hard to believe. Then again, she, in general, was hard to believe.

Her room was full of bands and singers and fashion pages

torn out of magazines, all haphazardly stuck to the white wall, quotes she'd scribbled in fat sharpie on lined loose leaf, and a collection of small ceramic ballet figurines.

I picked one up off her dresser.

"My mom was a ballerina in the opera."

Smoothing my thumb over a chip on the blonde bun, I wondered if ballerinas even did operas.

I set it down and read the quote nearest me, out loud: *"She left pieces behind her wherever she went—"*

"It's easier to feel the sunlight without them, she said." Ivy piled a stack of magazines on her bed and patted the spot next to her, but I kept reading.

"Someone I love gave me a box full of darkness. Are these from your songs?"

Shaking her head, she ripped open the bag of chips and offered it to me. I sat down on the edge of her bed and grabbed a few. Normally, I wouldn't think twice about having a burger for lunch and chips for a snack, but now I wasn't sure my body could handle both in one day.

"So, you're pretty into Hawk?" she asked, while crunching on a mouthful of crispy salt.

"Yeah," I admitted.

"Good. He's pretty into you, too."

"How long have you and Tony been together?"

"I don't even know. Since the band started. Hawk and I, on the other hand, have been together forever. Forever and forever more."

Well, that wasn't too hard to compete with.

"Our moms were neighbors when they had us. There's a picture of us on a couch at like one month, Hawk's hand all creepin' up my thigh. They used to tease us so bad." She rolled her eyes but the grin on her face didn't necessarily match the sentiment. "Anyway, I owe him almost everything. He's the one who got me singing."

"Because of his poems?"

"No. There was this huge tree house in his backyard that we started sleeping in when we were maybe eight. On weekends at first, because my mom hardly came home on weekends, and his brother would bring us cold hot dogs and candy canes. Hank had candy canes all year, always. I'd sing into them, but only ever in that tree house. Then after he got sent away, Hawk was so sad, I told him I'd do anything to cheer him up. He asked me to join choir." She popped a chip into her mouth. "So I did. Then a year later I got kicked out for coming on to the teacher, so Jay said we should start a band."

"You came on to Mr. Jung?" Mr. Jung was the high school choir director, and was so ancient I'd be surprised he wouldn't have had a heart attack had she hit on him.

"No, in seventh grade. Mr. Larson." She put a hand over her heart and threw herself back on the bed.

"You came on to a teacher in seventh grade?" This could not have actually happened.

She sat back up. "What can I say? He had lips that dreams are made of. I was determined they'd be my first." With a shrug, she flipped open a magazine. "Then in middle school everyone thought Hawk and I were together—we weren't, he just protected me from... well, from myself."

The foundation of my world was spinning. This girl had lived more in her life, and had more stories, than I probably ever would. Not that I'd hoped making out with teachers or getting kicked out of anything would be in my future, but still.

I grabbed the next magazine off the pile, and once I started, I couldn't stop. It was like art and beauty and all I'd ever wanted to be.

Pretty soon my fingers were greasy, my stomach full, and my eyes hungry like they'd never been before. My magazine experience was pretty nonexistent, but what I'd paged through in the grocery checkout were ones with articles on dating, quizzes about what kind of whatever you were in bed, and interviews with celebrities. Ivy was into something else altogether—high fashion stacked with thick, glossy pages and saturated with color. Fabrics shaped into form-fitting sculptures, a tribute to the female body.

Ivy's kind of body anyway. Spindly—they were extreme like she was extreme.

I glanced down at my cleavage, at the curve of my thigh, and wondered, once again, which kind of girl Hawk really preferred.

"You get it, right?" she asked softly. Reaching back, she pulled her hair over one shoulder and twisted it into a column. I looked into her huge pale eyes, and felt it, how Ivy Lang, of all people, was waiting for my approval.

With a nod, I gave it.

She patted her column of hair, let it go, and flipped to another page. "You can take some of my old ones home if you want."

"My mom might not like that."

She laughed a little.

"I'm serious. She's all about self-acceptance and loving your body."

"What does that have to do with anything?"

I played with the corner of a page that she'd dog-eared, a spread with one model and four men. "She thinks these models starve themselves."

"Not *all* of them. Anyway, who cares? Do you want some or not?"

"Yes." I wanted some.

She slid off her bed and pulled out an even bigger stack from the end table. "These are my favorites. The pages marked are how I want to feel when I'm on stage. I know I don't dress as classy as this or anything, but the intention is there, you know? I have to see what I'm being, what I'm putting out there."

I was set and ready to devour all of them.

"Tell me next time I remind you of one, okay?"

"Sure."

"It's all about the presentation, Eden." She squinted hard at the page, pressing her hand down flat on it. "Sometimes I think that's all I ever am, is the presentation."

13

Walking into the house, I held my backpack tightly beneath my arm. I stopped in the foyer, inhaled the scent of roasted chicken, and tried to guess where my mom might be. Not that she checked my homework anymore, but I felt like I was bringing contraband into the house.

Reese's face popped out from the hall, his shoulders relaxing when he saw me. "I thought you were going to be him."

"Excited?" I asked, still clutching my bag.

He shrugged.

"Where's Mom?"

He pointed toward the kitchen, and I nodded once before marching to my room and closing the door behind me.

I was pretty sure Reese had followed me and was waiting on the other side, but I had to hide the magazines before I did anything else.

The glossy pages spilled out as I released the zipper, and I looked around. My room stared back with a bored, empty face. Sure, there were volleyball medals hanging off old swim team trophies, and honors certificates propped up against pictures of me and my brother, me and Billie, me and my mom and Grandpa. The walls were the softest green, a color I'd picked, but there were no real hints to who I was that someone couldn't already see from the outside.

"Eden?" my brother asked, muffled like his lips were up against the crack of the door.

"One sec!" Slipping the magazines under the cushion of the window seat, I wondered where to find quotes like Ivy's, but ones that better fit me. Hurrying over, I opened the door on him. He was in his nicest clothes—his Christmas church clothes—and had brushed his hair down with a wet brush. "You look very handsome."

Shifting from one foot to the other, he mumbled a thanks, and I put my arm around him to lead him toward the kitchen.

My mom was whistling in front of the stove, stirring a risotto. The chicken I'd smelled when I came in was on the table, next to a new vase with a few sprigs of greens clipped from a bush out back.

The scent of her perfume wove its way through the onions and poultry. I glanced at my jeans and t-shirt, then at her nicest work dress, and decided I'd better change. But as I hit the little hall where the living room and kitchen met, a firm knock thumped the front door. Pivoting on my heels, I looked back. My brother was setting the table and my mom had her hands on not only the pot of rice, but also the oven door. She always said she could only do two things at a time.

Right. Whatever. I looked like a normal teenage girl instead of a kid dressing up for her new daddy (insert thick layer of sarcasm). Another knock and I was there, door open.

His hair was as carefully formed as my brother's and his nose as perfect as my mom's. A little belly and hairy hands, one of which was reaching out to me. "You must be Eden."

I shook it and nodded.

"I'm Jerry. Nice to finally meet you."

"You, too." I smiled.

He grinned back. Perfect teeth and a dimple that popped up on his right cheek.

"I hear you're a master swimmer," he said. "I was on the dive team, myself."

"I don't do that anymore."

"Don't swim?"

"Volleyball is my drug of choice now." Then I almost choked. "Not drug, I mean, sport. You know the phrase, I—"

"Baseball is my drug of choice now," he replied. "And I totally know what you mean." He scratched his neck, where his shirt was unbuttoned at the top. No tie. Or he'd lost it for dinner.

"Eden," my mom scolded from behind me, as she dried her hands on a dish towel. "Let him in, already."

Realizing I stood in his way, I slid over to let him pass.

He took the carpet in four long strides and wrapped one arm around my mom to settle a kiss on her nose. "You look lovely, Janie."

She went by Jane; she felt it carried more authority. So how close were they, exactly, if he was calling her Janie?

"Thank you," she said, her hands fluttering to her apron as she turned to disappear into the kitchen. "Jerry, this is Reese. Reese, I'd like you to meet Jerry."

It was stupid to change at this point, now that he'd seen me, so I swung into the bathroom to check my teeth and hair. I swished some water around in my mouth and spit it out, my hands bracing the sink.

My grandpa had been the last person to call her Janie, and with an unexpected kick, I was missing him like crazy.

"A ship is safest in harbor, but that's not what ships are for." Grandpa's voice resonated in my mind, the William Shedd quote he'd recited so often. Sometimes, he'd whisper it in my ear, or shout it across the room at my brother, or take my mom's hand and deliver it firmly.

I used to think he was being silly. Safety was all I'd wanted. But now I rushed to my room to write it down before it left me. My letters were shaky, hurried, but I needed to get it up there.

Scavenging through my desk for tape, I only found a few scattered pins. They'd have to do. Spinning around in the middle of my room, I searched for the best spot, clambered up on my window seat, and stuck it to the wood strip that ran down the center.

My mom's heels clicked her presence in the hallway, so I hurried to get down and meet her at the door.

"Eden, what on earth are you doing?" Her frown—oh, that

frown. "We have company. You're just going to disappear on a night like tonight?"

"I'm sorry, I'm coming."

She spun around and marched back to the kitchen. I hurried after her, took a deep breath, and slid into my seat.

~

Reese and I did the dishes while Jerry and my mom finished off their bottle of wine, then I helped Reese with his piano while they said goodbye on the porch.

When my mom came back inside, she was glowing: flushed cheeks, bright eyes, big smile. "So, what'd you think?" she asked.

"I liked him." I looked down at Reese, elbowing him. "What about you?"

He nodded, his fingers still going.

With a grin to my mom, I said, "We liked him."

She plopped down on the couch. "I was so nervous. But it went so well, don't you think? Don't you think it went well?"

I spun on the piano bench to face her. "Did he like us?"

"Of course he liked you."

The notes stopped. "I'm going to take my shower," Reese said.

I checked my watch while my mom craned her neck to see the clock on the microwave. "Oh my," she said. "I didn't realize dinner went so long."

"Dinner?" I teased. "Or the goodbye?"

She laughed, soft and quick, and Reese headed for the bathroom. I stood. "I should do my homework." She was looking out the window anyway, with a whisper of a smile on her face, so I left her with her thoughts.

As soon as I got my stuff out and organized, though, she was at my door. "Do you think Reese liked him?"

"Of course."

"He hardly ate anything. And he hardly said a word. Would you talk to him? Make sure?"

"Mom, he's fine. Why wouldn't he like him? It's not like he was offensive."

She walked over to sit on my window seat, and I noticed a shiny corner of magazine sticking out one inch from her leg. I froze.

"Maybe it's too soon for me to be doing this," she said.

Forcing myself to focus on her and not the contraband, I replied, "It's not too soon. If anything, it's been too long."

She leaned back and the tip of her head hit the paper I'd pinned up earlier. Reaching behind her, she twisted around, bracing her other hand one centimeter from the glossy pages beneath her.

The cushion slid out and a magazine fell to the ground. She kept reading the quote I'd posted, and I willed her not to look at the floor. I considered how obvious it would be if I ran over to pick it up or kick it under the bed.

"That's new," she finally said. "Does that mean Jerry reminded you of Grandpa?"

"He called you Janie."

She turned back to me. "He's right, you know, we were always too safe about everything."

"I know." That was the one thing I'd already figured out.

Her eyes fell to the waifish woman on the cover at her feet, the slit up the side of her dress, the smooth hair pulled severely into a ponytail.

I held myself still.

Reaching down for it, she asked, "What is this?"

"Nothing. A friend gave it to me." It came out too fast.

Her eyebrow went up. "Why were you hiding it?"

"I wasn't."

She crossed her arms, the magazine in one hand, under her armpit now. "This is garbage."

"It's fashion."

"It's impossible to live up to."

"It's fashion!"

"It's expectation!"

"But it's not even mine!"

"I don't care. I don't like you hiding things."

"I only hid it because I knew you wouldn't like it."

"Of course I wouldn't like it. But mostly, I don't like you hiding things." She stood to lift the cushion, revealing the others. Throwing the one in her hand on top of them, she said, "We are not made like those women, Eden, and that's okay. But the more you look at them, the more you're going to forget what matters and put all your energy into something that's not worth the fight."

"Don't you ever wish, though?" It was an incomplete question, I knew, but I couldn't bring myself to finish it. If she didn't know what I was talking about, then we weren't going to have this conversation. If she had never been where I was, then I was too embarrassed to explain.

"Sure. Of course. But honey, the fifty pounds I have on those models? It's my extra bits of happy—celebrating you, your brother, good games, successful recitals, birthdays. I'm okay with that. In fact, I'd choose it all over again, any day of the week." My mom stood up and walked to the door. "Don't let yourself get trapped, Eden, please."

"You're not going to take them?"

She crossed her arms tight. "You're old enough to make your own bad decisions, and you obviously know how I feel. I don't see that there's much more I can do." With a frown that made me shiver, she stalked out of the room.

I sat there, biting my lip and sitting on my crossed fingers, not sure what to do or think or say, yet feeling like I needed to apologize for not thinking the same things she did, which was like apologizing for my very self, my very thoughts. I sat like that until she came stalking back in with her own paper and pin.

She marched over to where I'd stuck my grandpa's quote and added one of her own: *"Comparison is the thief of joy." - Teddy Roosevelt.* Then she marched back out.

Releasing my fingers, I pulled my hands out from under me. And as Reese walked past my room to his, closing the door behind him for the night, I picked up my phone and called Billie.

"I have fashion magazines," I spit out when she answered.

"What?"

"Ivy gave me some high fashion magazines. You know, like the ones without articles? And this guy my mom brought home tonight—"

"Yeah, how'd it go?"

"I miss my grandpa."

"Your grandpa was awesome."

"I know." I chewed on my lip, feeling like I was gathering secrets and how wrong that felt. How far I felt from Billie with them between us. But I couldn't explain the magazines to her any more than I could've to my mom. "Also, Billie, I look amazing."

"Well, I wouldn't know, would I? Because you ditched us for lunch."

Oh. "I'm sorry. I needed a burger."

"Lame, Eden. If you're going to ditch us, at least be honest about it."

"I'm going to have lunch with Hawk sometimes, okay?"

"I don't care about that. I care that you didn't tell us you weren't coming. That we waited for you. That we saw you leaving the parking lot and Wes got all sad. That Isaac's mom was so excited it was the four of us, and then we walked in, *not* the four of us."

I chewed on my lip. "How would she have felt if it were five of us?" I wondered.

"You can't bring Hawk to Isaac's."

"Why not? I thought you liked him. You two were going on about straws for, like, an hour."

"I like him, sure. But what's he doing with his life?"

"Well, you wouldn't even know, would you? Have you asked?"

A silence stretched out, then a heavy sigh. "Fine, you win. I'm being an ass."

"Okay, so can I tell you a secret then?"

"Yes. Go."

"Back to me looking amazing. What I mean is I lost ten pounds and grew some more hair and my lips are bigger and my nose is smaller and—"

"Eden, that's impossible."

"I know. But Billie, I swear it happened. Last week I woke up looking different."

"Have you weighed yourself?"

"No. But it's not just that."

"You look the same."

"My mom noticed. That first morning, when I asked her, she said my clothes seemed stretched out, but they were new."

"Moms are all about humoring us. Did she want you to do something?"

"No. Just eat breakfast."

"Exactly. Listen, things like that don't happen. They just don't. Your mind is playing tricks on you."

"What tricks? One day I hate how I look and the next I don't?"

"Give me a break, you never hated how you looked."

"I did."

"You did not."

"I did!"

"You have a problem."

"Billie, you're not helping me."

She sighed. I could almost feel the whoosh through the phone. "I'm sorry. What do you want me to say?"

Sometimes the problem with having a strong friend was that they didn't believe in bullshit. They didn't believe in pumping you up. And they didn't believe in crazy things, either. They believed in fact.

"I don't know what I want you to say," I admitted.

The lights went out in the hall, a sign my mom had said good night to my brother, and the TV clicked on in the living room. She'd watch the news and then read in bed. Everyone was settling down, and yet I felt completely unsettled.

Finally, Billie broke the silence. "Did you find something for your psych paper yet?"

"What?"

"You know, for this perception unit. Maybe your topic should be you."

"You mean that list we're supposed to make?"

"Did you make it?"

"No." I flipped open my binder. "I haven't done anything for psych since the Weber's law thing."

"I think you should make it about yourself," she repeated.

"I was actually considering it." My gaze fell on my mom's quote, and I decided it was maybe time to weigh myself. Billie thought I was crazy and I was starting to worry she was right, but if I'd actually lost ten pounds, I could prove I wasn't.

Then again, if I stepped on that scale, the carriage might morph back into a pumpkin and trap me inside again, insecure forever. And regardless, weight loss wouldn't explain the little things—the hair and the nose and the lips. But enough of this, I had to know.

"I'm coming over," I announced, interrupting her. She'd been talking about her list, the one she'd made extra, not for the project, but on Isaac. "Can I come over?"

"What?"

"I need to weigh myself."

"Yeah, it's fine. Come over." Her dad had MS, so on some

days, when he didn't want anyone to witness his pain or weakness, visitors weren't allowed. "Have you been listening to anything I said?"

I slipped on my shoes and grabbed an old history paper from my desk, told my mom I was going to Billie's to drop off something important, and rushed out the door, all while still on the phone.

"Eden!" Billie jerked my attention back to her.

"Yes! I've been listening. And you forgot his ultimate defining characteristic."

"Which is what?"

"His insane need to spout the truth. Which is totally both a positive *and* a negative."

"Mm. That is good." I could hear her chewing on her pencil and pictured her on her bed—legs crossed, books and papers spread in front of her, light off but lamp glowing, music on but barely discernible, maybe an energy drink within reach.

Three short minutes later, her mom let me in the house and I ran up the stairs to find her exactly like that, only the energy drink cans (three of them) were empty and tossed on the hardwood floor.

"Hi," I said, finally hanging up on her. "I'll be right back." Then I made my way to the bathroom.

Closing the door, I took a deep breath. This was it. The truth revealed: rapid weight loss, or magic exists.

One foot, two feet, and a hand on the towel rack to brace

myself.

The digital reading did its thing, and I stood there staring as it beeped.

I'd lost only 1.3 pounds since the last time I'd weighed myself. And maybe my sanity.

Tuesday

I studied my list—my personal pros and cons—as Mr. Keller went on and on about perception and focus, and how focusing our energy could change our perception.

"Anais Nin said, 'We don't see things as they are. We see them as we are.'" He paused to look up at the speckled ceiling as if this wisdom had come straight from God.

A week ago, I'd have rolled my eyes over to Billie for a shared moment, but today I scribbled that quote down, since I was collecting them.

Dropping his gaze, he crossed his arms. "That's another way to say there are two sides to every story—three, actually. Your side, the other person's side, and the objective actuality. So, you see, if you tell yourself the same thing over and over—wherever you may have taken it from in the first place is no matter—if you keep thinking one way, that will be your reality. However,"—dramatic pause—"I propose that you can change your reality." He clicked on the SMART Board. "I give you my wife's cat."

It was adorable: long, flowing white hair with a caramelized brown spot on the side of its ear.

"Don't let his looks fool you. He's naughty. I hated him. When my wife and I were dating, I couldn't stand to be in the same room as him. Granted, I'd always been a dog person, but he was also a jerk. Anyway, she held that against me, and when I proposed, she said I'd be marrying him too. She wanted to know if I could stand to live with him for ten more years, until he died and she got another cat that I hated, and then could I stand to live with *that* cat for another eigh*teen* years. See where I'm going with this?

"So I promised her I'd get used to cats, and I started forcing myself, for every bad thing I thought, to think a good thing. Sure, his litter box stinks, but he's pretty. Sure, he chews on my shoes like a dog, but he's funny when there's a small box or paper bag around. Sure, he sleeps on the bed, but he keeps me company when my wife is gone on business trips. And, as she always said, at least he didn't sleep on my pillow, like her last cat would have.

"Know what happened?" Mr. K waited, but none of us raised our hands. "I ended up loving that dang cat. When he died on us three years later, I was a mess. And now we have a new cat, just like she said we would, but I still miss this stupid thing so bad it hurts." He cleared his throat. "Point is, guys, I forced myself to see the other side of the coin."

Checking the clock, he moved back to his desk.

"We have about fifteen more minutes. I want you to take that and memorize your list. Then, every time one of those negatives pops into your head, I want you to stop yourself and recite the positive. Over and over, for the next four weeks, until you can actually see the good in this something you previously hated. And at the end of those four weeks, I want a paper on what you've learned. Were you able to change how you thought, specifically? Or in general, did you find yourself empathizing more with other people, because of the practice? Whatever it is, write about it, all right?"

His *all rights* were really requests for nods, so a few of us obliged. Then he sat down behind his desk and pulled a book out while we went at our lists.

Mine was on a random inner page of my notebook, and I shielded it with my hair, the notebook cover, and my arm.

NEGATIVE:	POSITIVE:
Thick legs	Strong
Ugly knees	No one has pretty knees
"Cheeks"	Some people get surgery for curves
Soft arms	Can do something about this
Bulbous nose	Okay, so it's not really bulbous
Crooked tooth	It doesn't actually stick out

Did it count if everything on my list was better since I'd woken up perfect? Well, except my front teeth, which sort of leaned into each other. Maybe I should do it on my grandpa's watch after all.

Billie poked me with her foot, which had snuck its way across the aisle. She motioned that she wanted to swap, her list for mine.

I closed the notebook and shook my head. She raised her brow and motioned again. Though it would be interesting to see the pros and cons on Isaac, I mouthed *no*.

She ripped a page out of her composition book, scribbled on it, and handed it to me: *Did you put your impossibly white teeth on there?*

I texted her back: *No, you were only supposed to list your negatives.*

She got out her phone and immediately had a reply: *Maybe for the assignment, but for the sake of your self-esteem, you should look at your positives, too. Like your teeth. And your perfect fingernails. Plus, you're funny and smart and athletic. Someday you're going to take over the world. Who cares what the scale says?*

I stared at her words, wondering why I'd only thought to make a list of physical attributes, then replied, *The scale says I'm a nutcase.*

But you're my nutcase. And Wes's nutcase. And Isaac's nutcase. And we love you like crazy. So it's all good.

I closed my eyes and took a deep, leveling breath in, wondering what Hawk saw in me.

More importantly, what did I see in myself? And when had I stopped seeing anything but that which showed up in the mirror?

Clenching my teeth, I flipped through the pages, back to middle, and added:

Crooked tooth	~~It doesn't actually stick out~~ Impossibly white
Not delicate	ATHLETIC & GRACEFUL
Timid	Not naïve – thinks twice.

15

Hawk was waiting at my locker after school, something he'd done a few days in a row now. I smiled as I made my way through the thinning hallway to him, grinning bigger as I worked my combination lock.

He leaned his shoulder against the metal and slid closer to me. "Mr. Brault told me today that I shouldn't tug at the ankles of those on top of the ladder."

I frowned. "He wasn't talking about me."

"He most certainly was."

"He couldn't have been."

"He's never bothered to speak to me in the past."

"It's not like he particularly likes me."

"Are you sure? Aren't you a genius in math?"

"I mean, base level genius. Not anything special genius."

The side of his mouth lifted up. "Your arrogance is cute."

"What? It's not like it's that hard, math. If people wanted to do better—"

He cut me off with a snort. "Okay, Ms. Genius."

I packed up my bag and closed the locker door. "That's awful. We should report him."

"For what? For trying to protect you?"

"For making judgments and not caring about each of his

students the same."

Hawk raised an eyebrow. "That's cute, too," he said.

I deepened my frown and narrowed my eyes for good measure. "I suppose I should be happy that someone finds my arrogance and naiveté cute."

"Don't you have volleyball?" a voice asked, louder than normal and harsher than necessary.

We stepped away from each other to find Wes, with hands on his backpack straps. We'd been standing awfully close to each other, I'd give him that.

"Don't you have swim?" I countered.

"Yes." He looked from me to Hawk and back. "And what does he have?"

"He has not-being-a-jerk," I snapped. "I know your mom taught you to speak directly to people when they're standing in front of you." Then, looking back to Hawk, I asked, "What's with everyone today? Are they all like this?"

The smirk I got in return was not the sexy, amused type, but the yeah-I'm-not-surprised kind. "Pretty much."

I kind of wanted to get back at Wes for that, not to mention make Hawk feel better about all these assumptions people made of him, so I slipped my face against his neck and took a quick, heavenly breath in, kissing him there as quickly and softly as I could.

Pulling back, I gave Hawk a small, sad smile. "I'll call you when I'm done." Then I shoved past Wes, caught sight of Nat and Javi down the hall, and hurried to catch up.

Crashing between them, I looped an arm through each of theirs, noting how their chattering went silent.

"Talking about me?" I asked.

"Just this weekend," Javi said.

"What about this weekend?"

Their glances skipped off mine and found each other. It was like that sometimes. They were best friends, and though volleyball pulled us together, we didn't hang out aside from that.

"Fine, don't tell me."

"You wouldn't like it," Nat said.

"What would I possibly not like?" I asked as we swung into the locker room. "Are you planning a murder?"

She grinned. "Just a bank heist."

"What's the big deal then?" Though honestly, my stomach was going a little sideways. Maybe I didn't want to know.

"She is with Hawk now, maybe she's loosened up a little." That was Javi, talking over my head as we started braiding each other's hair.

"I'm loose," I agreed. "In fact, I'm going to a party this weekend."

Nat turned to me with raised eyebrows.

"What? Why so surprised?"

"You can be kind of..."

"Kind of judgmental," Javi finished.

"Kind of a prick about people not being perfect."

"Not true!" I cried. "You can do whatever you want!"

"Except we know it would make you nervous."

"Yeah, and you'd be all worried about us and scold us and stuff."

"Wait. Does that mean you don't tell me things on a regular basis?"

Silence.

"What kind of shit have you gotten into?" I cried, my voice almost squeaky. Yes, I'd used a swear word on purpose to make a point.

"We've gotten into mostly mild shit," Nat admitted.

"Moderate on very few occasions."

"I mean, obviously you've been to a party." I wasn't an idiot. But if we were caught at a party, or a picture showed up on social media, we'd be kicked off the team. Javi couldn't afford that.

"Know what else?" Javi asked, then leaned forward to whisper in my ear. "We've vaped."

"Vaping will kill your brain before it's fully developed." I'd spit that out before I could catch it.

"There she is again," Javi said, with a pat to my shoulder. I bit my lip and finished Nat's hair before Javi finished mine.

Nat turned to me with a grin. "Next time we'll smoke pot. Better?"

"Weed kills your motivation." Oh, I could kick myself.

"Sorry. I'm sorry."

Javi banded my braid, then wrapped her arms around my neck and leaned her chin on my shoulder. "We get you're you, Eden. We love you anyway."

They glanced at each other again, the same look as earlier, which meant something was in their heads and they didn't plan on sharing it with me. This time, though, I think I heard it. They wanted me to be okay with all of who they were, the same way they were okay with me being all of who I was. Even if we weren't the same.

I'd glued myself to people who were exactly like me—or I'd formed myself to fit with them. If I hadn't been who I was—or who Billie was—maybe I'd be closer with Nat and Javi. Even if not present while they did those things, maybe I'd have heard about it. I wanted to be me in a way that still let them be them. It shouldn't have to be an either/or.

"But, if you get caught…"

They waved it off. "Yeah, no one gets caught."

I let out a slow breath. "Come to Ivy's party. I'll send you the address, okay?"

"Sure." Nat smiled and reached for my hand. Sometimes we led each other out to the gym like this.

Javi skipped along beside us. "Will we get to see you and Hawk make out again?"

They'd catcalled Hawk and I after lunch, after witnessing one very proper, closed-mouth kiss. "Please, have you seen

Gina and David lately?"

Nat put an arm up to her face and opened her mouth as wide as it would go.

"More drool," Javi said. "You need more tongue and more drool."

"Also, where are the roaming hands?" I asked.

"Yeah, geez, you're totally not doing it right."

Nat dropped her arm. "I guess I need more practice."

Javi made random kissy faces at her—or possibly both of us—as we entered the gym. I pulled in a deep breath, the scent filling and buoying me like always.

Coach clapped his hand on my shoulder, no escaping this time. "Eden," he barked. "I need you to commit today."

I turned, loosening his hold, and walked backwards. "I'm committed!"

As soon as he moved his attention elsewhere, I muttered, "I've always been committed."

"I think you lost some focus is all," Nat said. "New boys do that."

"Just don't forget State is on the line," Javi added.

I high-fived her. "This is our year." Only it came out weak, because if it was our year, we couldn't stand to lose many more games.

And I hadn't been much help lately.

Saturday

Wanna come to a party? I asked our group chat.

Isaac: *Lol.*

Wes: *Can't we just café instead?*

When he used café as a verb, it meant the one that was open late, where we stuffed our faces with pastries. Sometimes, we'd bet each other we couldn't finish all that was left in the case, and sometimes, someone would end up puking.

Not terribly unlike a normal high school party, only without the alcohol.

I twirled my watch on my wrist and remembered how poorly it had gone with Isaac and Hawk that first night. Adding Wes to the mix probably wasn't the best idea, and Billie was simply not answering, so I wouldn't push it.

I'm going to the party.

I sent them the address, in case they changed their mind, then sent it to Javi and Nat too. Dropping my phone on the bed,

I stood in front of my closet and contemplated what kind of outfit a girl who went to parties would wear. It wasn't easy, considering I'd never been that type of girl before. But now I was also trying to prove to my friends—my less judgmental friends—that I was cool with whatever bad decisions they felt like making.

What do you wear to a party? I asked Ivy.

Just come oooooooverrrrr, she replied. *I will get you ready.*

But I was supposed to go to Billie's thing first. Only I'd been to a million trillion of them and not one party in my entire existence.

Okay, that wasn't exactly true. We'd walked into one sophomore year. The four of us, nearly arm in arm, and Isaac had promptly walked out. Wes followed him the moment someone took a picture and seemed to be uploading it on social media. They waited on the front lawn for us to decide it wasn't our scene either, which had only taken Billie as long as one look into the living room where people were acting like idiots, but she trailed around after me until I almost got sprayed with beer. Some kid spit it out, choked on it almost, and it reached the tips of my shoes.

Then there was Nat's birthday party junior year. They'd invited me. I said I was going. I chickened out because Billie, Wes, and Isaac hadn't been invited, and I didn't want to walk in alone.

Supposedly, it had been epic. A rager. I might have wrinkled my nose the entire time they told me about it. So yeah, it was all starting to make sense now.

Hawk picked me up and when we arrived, Ivy immediately went at my eyes. Ten layers of mascara and some heavy eyeliner later, plus a borrowed shirt that wouldn't stop falling off my shoulder (*That's the point*, Ivy said), and I was deemed ready for the party.

"My bra does not work with this shirt," I said, standing in front of her mirror.

"Then take it off. Who needs a bra?"

I blinked. I needed a bra, that was who. Only, really, wasn't braless the feminist thing? I bent over, testing how much you could see. I'd have to hold my shirt to my chest either way.

"So don't bend over," Ivy said. "Or just don't worry about it."

Just don't worry about it. Maybe that was my problem—the difference between her and me, or between her and who I'd been. She didn't worry about what was coming, didn't try to control the outcome. I slipped off my bra and studied myself again.

"Stop futzing." Grabbing my hand, she tugged me out of her room. "Let's get snacks."

As we swung through the living room, I startled at a figure on the deck. It was only Tony, smoking a cigarette. As we rounded the island into the kitchen, he saw us and pressed his forehead up against the window.

"Has he been out there this whole time?" I asked.

She handed me two half bags of potato chips and a big plastic bowl. "He's mad at me. Wants me to beg for his forgiveness."

"Why's he mad at you?"

"Some fanboy asked me to sign his butt. Dropped trou right there and handed me a sharpie. So I did, and I invited him to the party tonight. Which means he,"—she jerked a hand in the direction of the balcony—"thinks I want a new boyfriend."

"Do you?"

"Only if Hawk were free." She winked and then, before I had time to even think about how to respond, corrected herself. "Kidding! But I will do anything for my fans."

As I mixed the chips together, Tony slid down to a crouch. He was now crumpled in the corner, cheek resting on the glass.

It would've made an awesome pic, the kind that would end up in some big city art gallery—his melodrama accented by the completely neutral palette, but for his navy baseball hat. White walls, soft gray sky, hard gray decking, washed out jeans, charcoal hoodie.

"It must be so weird to have fans."

"I don't have very many."

"Sure you do." They drew a decent crowd, and Hawk said people randomly came up to her sometimes. Plus, "I'm your fan."

She grinned. "Aw. You're pretty lovely yourself, you know?"

"Most of the time I don't, actually."

Ripping open a huge bag of popcorn, she sighed. "That's why I need fans. Because I don't either."

The door started banging and Ivy nodded for me to open it. Jay and Hawk had a keg between them and one off to the side. She held the door open as they brought them both in, and then all there was to do was wait.

I checked my magic watch, which hadn't been working at all lately, either because it had been in the shower too much or because it was working on me and not the time. I looked at Hawk. "Maybe we should go to Billie's thing."

"Or we could order pizza," Ivy said, now with a myriad of bowls in front of her, crowding the counter.

Remembering the eye liner and the fact that I wasn't wearing a bra, I nodded. "Pizza sounds good."

After that was ordered, Ivy finally went outside to deal with Tony, and Jay sat down at the table to wrap the shoebox people would put their beer money in.

I wandered over to the keg and plastic cups. "Okay, show me how this works."

"Can't yet," Hawk said, following me. "It's supposed to sit a bit before we tap it."

"Before you what it?"

That grin of his, I didn't even care if he was laughing at my ignorance, it lit up his face like I'd seldom seen on a person. "You have to let it sit after moving it, because it's all shaken up. Then you tap it—screw this in." He picked up the handle thing on the counter. "Then run through the foam."

"You know a lot about beer for someone I've never seen drink."

He lifted one shoulder. "I had a girlfriend who said there was nothing worse than kissing someone who smelled like alcohol."

I smiled. "Planning on doing a lot of kissing tonight?"

He set the tap down but kept his hand on it. "Any kissing at all and I wouldn't want to smell like beer."

"What if we smelled like beer together?"

"Then who would bring you home?"

"Well, now I feel like I can't drink."

"Why do you have to?"

"I don't." I set a hip against the counter, close to his hand. "But I want to."

"Really?"

I let myself think about this for a minute. But yes, really. The whole point of all this magic (that might not really be magic) was that I wanted to try out someone else. If I didn't actually want to drink, I at least wanted to know what it felt like. I also didn't want Javi and Nat to keep things from me anymore. They were coming, and we were drinking, and then they'd understand I wasn't the prissy, judgmental friend they'd assumed me to be.

I had a sober ride home, and I was in a safe place with people I trusted. When better?

"Yes, really."

With the slightest twitch at the edge of his mouth, Hawk stepped in closer and kissed me. He kissed me while Ivy and Tony screamed at each other on the other side of the closed sliding glass door, and he kissed me while Jay got serious at the table with colored markers, only a few feet away.

He kissed me, then showed me how to tap the keg, then kissed me, then we emptied the foam. I started to fill a cup for myself, but he stopped me halfway.

"Start slow. Maybe stay slow too, until you know how you handle it." As he spoke, I took steady sips from the cup and watched him over the rim. "And how much you can handle." He gave me a look and I laughed.

"Yeah, yeah," I agreed. "Okay."

But slow was not how Javi and Nat did it. In fact, my eyes about bugged out of my head as Nat drained her first cup in almost an instant. Not to mention, I hardly recognized them in party getup. Then again, I wouldn't be caught dead at school with no bra and this eyeshadow. Javi was in a slinky red dress and her hair was loose of its braids, a cloud about her face. Though she was the tougher one on the court, Nat was apparently tougher in real life, with tights under frayed black shorts, a Blondie tee, and a quilted orange faux-leather jacket.

I suppose we *were* celebrating a Thursday night game win. By the skin of our teeth, but State would come to those who won whichever way.

Nat winked at me as she filled her cup again, and I corrected myself quickly. I was cool, and I was not judgmental—I had to keep reminding myself.

Then the buzz kicked in and I grinned widely, realizing *that's* why people called it a buzz—of course, it made so much sense—and suddenly, I really was cool and not judgmental. Everything was great and I was relaxed; my friends were there and we were dancing in the middle of the living room—I was dancing! Without thinking about it! In public!

Granted, it was tight in the living room. In the whole apartment, honestly. People swarmed; they were packed into the kitchen, stuffed around the kitchen table, spilling through the sliding door onto the little deck, even overflowing into the common areas of the building, out the hall, and down the stairs. It was a stew of high school kids I didn't recognize (probably not from our school), friends of Jay's, and fans ranging from our age to forty, some of whom were pretty creepy.

I wondered if the kids at school knew Ivy had so many fans. Maybe they wouldn't ignore her if they did.

Then she was there, twirling me, dancing with Javi, Nat, and I. Hawk was perched on the arm of the couch, talking to some hairy guy with a snarled beard.

Like Ivy created space for herself wherever she went, to do what she wanted, it felt like I'd created the space in the living room. A handful of others moved with us, and the crowd lapped around us like waves on a beach.

Then the tide rolled in, bringing Billie and Isaac and Wes with it.

"Hey!" I cried, lurching toward them with a beer in my hand. Now I was the type of girl who danced at a party with a beer in her hand. "You came!"

Wes put his hands up in front of him and Isaac stepped back. Billie wrinkled her nose.

"Come on! I'll get you a beer. I know how to pour a keg!" But when I put an arm around Billie to guide her toward the kitchen, she stepped back.

"We do not want beer," Isaac said.

I stared at them: one confused face, one disgusted, and one of disbelief. That broke the spell, and their disappointment pierced through the fog I'd been dancing in. I dropped my arms and tried to hide my cup behind me.

"Okay, well, wanna dance? We were dancing." Glancing around, I took a few steps to deposit my beer on the fireplace mantle.

"Where's Hawk?" Billie asked, as if he was her friend and not me. Her eyes followed mine, to where he was still perched on the couch. "Who's *that*?"

I shrugged. I didn't know half of these people.

Nat and Javi gave me looks, like, *See? See who you were?*

I swallowed, my tongue thick and sweaty, like it was coated with yeast, which might not be all that much off the mark, considering.

"Are you…?" Wes stammered. "Did you…?"

"Did I what?" I asked, now slightly irritated.

"Your eyes."

"You look like a raccoon," Isaac added.

I rolled them. "Here we go again."

Billie took a step toward me and whispered, "Do you even have a bra on?"

With a proud grin, I replied, "No. Aren't you proud of me?"

"Proud?" she hissed. "You know what that says to Hawk, right? To every guy in here?"

My skin went cold, but now Javi and Nat were standing next to me. They sipped beer out of their cups with perfect calm, as if they knew I needed people on my side. Like I was facing off against my lifelong best friends forever.

What was happening?

"It says I'm not conforming to some social construct invented by a man," I managed to reply.

Billie rolled her eyes. "Fine, but your *nipples*, Eden."

I looked down. The shirt was loose enough that my nipples were barely showing. But great. Now I had a complex. Marching off to Ivy's room, I snatched up my bra and slid back into it, maneuvering so I didn't need to take off my shirt. When I spun back around, Billie, Isaac, and Wes stood just inside the room. Javi and Nat were in the doorway, still sipping, and Hawk was pushing his way through.

"Everything okay?" he asked.

"Everything is *not* okay," Javi told him. "Eden was forced back into normalizing her breasts in order to avoid taunting the male species. The male species, which has determined the onus is on her to keep herself unattractive until the moment she decides she wants to be ravished."

We all stared at her.

"What?" She sipped at her beer. "Billie doesn't have the monopoly on feminism just because she wears the t-shirts."

"I..." Billie cleared her throat. "That's not what..."

I almost laughed at my best friend stammering, at having been bested by someone she was looking at with disdain.

"You know, Javi," Isaac narrowed his eyes at her. "You could get kicked off the volleyball team if someone saw you with that."

"No one is going to tell on her," Nat said, her tone as serious as her smoothed-back hair.

"Hey, cuties!" Ivy's voice preceded her, a generic call. "That room is off—oh." She stopped next to Hawk. "What's going on? Everything cool?"

"Everything's fine." I motioned them to move out. "Sorry."

"No, it's okay. My room isn't off limits to you."

"Eden, why don't you come with us?" Isaac, of course, because he was the most offended by a party scene.

"You need to sober up," Wes agreed. "Besides, did you see those creeps on the couch?"

Ivy stiffened. "Those are my creeps, thank you very much."

Wes raised an eyebrow at her. "Those old guys?"

"My uncle and his friends?"

"Isn't it a little weird that your uncle wants to come hang out with a bunch of high schoolers?" Billie asked.

"This isn't a high school party." Ivy's voice was now a close resemblance of the steel that Nat's had been. "It's just a party. Inclusive of all, but mostly for those who love our band. Do you love our band? Do you know what inclusive means?"

A silence spread, the beat of the music from the living room rumbling through our bodies, giving an echo to the tension.

"Stop," I said. This wasn't supposed to be how it happened. They were all supposed to get along. "Can we just start over?"

"Start over, how?" Isaac asked. "I'm not staying here." And out he went.

"Billie..." But she only looked at my shirt, at my bare shoulder—well, bare with a bra strap now.

Wes took a long look at Hawk. "You better get her home safe."

Considering the clip in his voice, I didn't blame Hawk for his reply. "Besides the fact that I'm not drinking, you're an ass."

"At least I'm not a loser," Wes muttered.

Javi stepped cleanly between them, which I'd have to thank her for later, because I was a bit shocked. That's the only way I could explain my speechlessness and inaction.

"At least I have the girl," Hawk said, wincing immediately after the words came out of his mouth. Yeah, not pretty. I slumped down on Ivy's bed.

"I think it's time for you to go," Ivy told Wes, but my head was spinning.

The room blurred, and the spinning dropped from my head to my stomach, as I realized the person I'd been. No wonder Javi and Nat didn't tell me things. I'd made it clear, as surely as my friends had just now, that if the story was doused with beer, or the characters shaded with a 3.0 GPA, I wouldn't approve.

Needing air, I pushed past them for the door. My hand touched down on each of them as I went, but there were only four. So Billie and Wes had gone after Isaac. Had left me sitting there with my hand on my stomach. Had not said goodbye.

I shoved past the people in the hall, along the edge of the mass in the living room, no longer dancing—shouting though, lots of shouting. I grabbed my beer back from the mantle, because far be it from me to be the type of girl who didn't pick up after herself, and wove my way out of the apartment and down the stairs. Someone was holding the front door of the building open, and someone was charging in. They knocked into me and I sloshed beer all over my shirt, then stumbled onto the large grassy area in front of the building.

Looking up at the inky sky, I blinked back a few tears.

Wes appeared, hand to my elbow. "Thank goodness. We thought you weren't coming."

Billie and Isaac stood on the curb where Isaac's SUV was

parked, hands together. Except Billie didn't hold hands. Not only because she wanted their relationship fluid and without definition, but because she believed it inferred ownership. She also never lost time pointing out how parents held children's hands in order to keep track of them, in check, and she refused to let someone else do that to her, or do that to someone else.

I ripped myself away from Wes, my stomach churning in disgust. Or beer. Hard to tell. "You guys are the worst, you know that?"

He scoffed. "Us? Really?"

I ran my hands over my face, the crumpled cup still in my grip and leaking beer onto my cheek. "I just wanted to go to a party. *With* you guys. I wanted everyone to get to know each other."

"We know enough."

Spoiled. My stomach spoiled. I was spoiled; they were spoiled. Sour. "What's that supposed to mean?"

Wes glanced over his shoulder to where someone was puking off the deck.

"That guy's not—that's not…" But that was Tony actually, and not only was he one of the people I'd been spending time with, but I myself had just recently stopped calling him Suckface in my head. "At least they do things and try things and live life, instead of standing still and trying to cover up their fear by being holier than thou, which just makes you look like assholes. No, on second thought, you *are* assholes. Honestly, I can't believe you're all such assholes. And I can't believe I let you pull me along for so long. That's what I'm over. That's what I'm done with."

I might have spit a little. I had to wipe my mouth.

Wes stiffened and began to turn, then spun back. "Clearly, you're going through something, and if you want to throw me aside, fine, but make it right with Billie. Her strength is what you need right now."

I pointed to my own chest. "*My* strength is what I need now. *Mine.*"

His gaze flicked over my shoulder toward the building, and I caught movement out of the corner of my eye. That, the stars, and my outburst had me a bit dizzy. Or maybe it was the alcohol I was so not used to.

"I'll study at home tomorrow," Wes said. "You don't have to worry about me stopping by anymore." And with that, off he went to Billie and Isaac, the three of them leaving me alone in the dark.

I managed to turn around just in time to double over and puke on a pair of very nice shoes. Covering my mouth in horror, I straightened.

"Eden?"

Oh, *shit.* "Jerry?"

"Eden." He stepped back, out of the muddy puddle that was regurgitated potato chips and foamy beer.

"Is there a problem here?" Hawk asked, circling Jerry to put an arm around my waist. I put a hand out to stop him from being territorial but it probably only looked like I was trying to steady myself.

There was a hard edge in Hawk's eyes as he assessed this stranger whose attention was on me, and a harder one in Jerry's as he sized up this rough-looking kid with his hands all over his girlfriend's goody-two-shoes daughter.

"The problem is Eden is underage and clearly drunk." Jerry glanced down to shake off his shoes. "Also alone in the middle of a dark, open space where lurkers like to lurk. Perhaps you are a lurker yourself." Slipping out of the shoe most covered with vomit, he crouched down to pick it up gingerly and wiped it off as best he could on the grass.

If only I had another t-shirt or something. I bit down on my knuckle, then said, "Hawk, this is my mom's boyfriend, Jerry. Jerry, my boyfriend, Hawk."

Jerry looked up in the midst of shaking off his hand. Oh, God, I hoped he didn't have vomit on his hand. "What are you doing here?" he asked.

Hawk answered, "Our friend is having a party."

"What are *you* doing here?" I countered. "Are you coming to the party?"

Jerry narrowed his eyes at me, as if I was being ridiculous. I tried to ignore the wet stink coming off my shirt. Or off Jerry's shoes.

"I live here," he said.

"Here?" I repeated. Because he was an attorney.

He eyed me for a second. "I haven't bothered to move since law school. I work too much and moving is the worst."

Okay, damage control. "I'm not drunk," I mumbled. "Just fighting with my friends. And bad sushi."

Jerry stood, one shoe in his hand. "This, all over me, is not sushi."

I tried to think, feeling like the cards were dangerously close to crashing around me. But the wind was picking up, whipping the tree limbs around, and whipping my thoughts around with it. At least my stomach was feeling better.

"I'll get her home," Hawk offered. "If that's all right with you, sir, I'll get her home now."

Jerry raised an eyebrow at him, and I decided he could make a very effective father figure, which would be awesome for Reese. Not for me though. I was past that.

"I'll allow it only because you don't smell like you've had a drop, and because I would like to change my shoes." He glanced at them. "But tomorrow, when your mother and I talk, she will know. So if you want to tell her first, you'd better do it tonight."

I resisted the urge to roll my eyes. Way to help a girl out.

As I beelined to the parking lot, it occurred to me what other adults I could have run into. My volleyball coach, for instance, who, with his salary, was more likely to live in a place like this than a lawyer. Javi and Nat said it didn't matter, but if he'd seen me himself, would he have let it slide? Or would I have been booted off the team? I swallowed the fluttering moth in my throat and slid into Hawk's car.

"You okay?" he asked, giving me a sideways glance as he started the engine. Admittedly, I was gasping a little for air.

"Next week, let's go to the movies."

I texted Ivy that I'd get my bag later, then texted Nat and Javi that I'd just thrown up on my mom's boyfriend so I was leaving. *Love you see you later.*

He backed out without turning the radio on. "Next week we *should* go to the movies."

I slumped in my seat and stared ahead. "What's that supposed to mean?"

Even though I was being insolent, he reached for my hand. "It means we haven't done a lot of your life. We've mostly just been doing mine."

"My life is lame, Hawk."

"I'm sure it's not."

"There's lots of studying—"

"I'll write."

"And swimming—"

"Swimming was my idea first."

"No beer or anything like that. Only sugar—"

"I can sugar with the best of 'em."

If I could have slumped more, I would've. "Except there's no *them* anymore because my friends are judgmental assholes." I turned to him. "Was I a judgmental asshole, all this time?"

He squeezed my hand. "Not actively."

"Were they? Could you tell?"

"I never paid attention."

"So yes, then."

"Maybe just Isaac."

"You're being too nice to me. To them." I took my hand from his. "Except, 'At least I have the girl'? Really?"

He tapped his fingertips along the steering wheel. "Yeah, I'm really sorry about that. It popped out, which isn't like me. It was just a dumb sucker punch."

"Well, I can't say he didn't deserve a sucker punch right about then."

"But you can't be had, I know that. I'm not trying to 'have' you."

"Or maybe I can be." I smiled a little. "I mean, you do have me."

Hawk parked at the curb in front of my house and took my hand again, twisting our fingers together and tugging me back to him. "We're okay, then?"

"We might be the only thing in my life that's okay."

"You're joking, right? You're, like, the golden girl."

I snorted. "I just realized my friends suck, I've been having problems with my game—though, I guess scholarships only care that I'm co-captain, right? They don't care how good I actually am? Like, they want to see the extra-curricular and leadership skills, that's the point, right?"

He made a face like scholarship committee decisions were as far beyond him as anything.

"Plus I just *puked* on my mom's boyfriend."

"Not a great time to come in and meet your mom then?" He smiled a little to let me know it was a joke.

I folded into a short laugh, thankful for him breaking the moment, and swung the car door open, leaving that as our goodbye.

The porch and hall light were on, but that was it. Otherwise it was quiet, the clock on the piano ticking, the fridge humming. Everything and everyone hushed and asleep, as if I was the type of girl who could be trusted to get home safe.

No need to wake my mom up and break her heart. Might as well let her get a good night's sleep. Locking up, I flipped off the lights and slid into bed still in Ivy's shirt.

Sunday

I woke up with an ache in my chest where my friends used to be. They might have been complete assholes the night before, but they were my assholes.

The way I figured it, as soon as I told my mom where I'd been and what I'd been doing, my life would be shut down, at least for the day. I got dressed, brushed my teeth and tongue no less than four times, then snuck into the kitchen for a banana. Hopefully I could get out of the house before Jerry got to my mom.

"Where are you going?"

I startled, but it was only Reese. He stood in the doorway, picking at a piece of chipped paint on the wooden frame. He'd been doing this for years, in various places around the house. I kind of loved him leaving his mark like that, but Mom did not.

Walking over, I placed my hand on his. "Billie's."

"Wes isn't coming over?"

"Not today." And according to him, never again.

Mom's door creaked open, and I leaned over to whisper in his ear. "Gotta go."

"You're up early," my mom noted, as she walked toward us in her bathrobe.

"Billie's. Big psych project." Thankful my backpack was right there in the entry, I grabbed it like it was proof. Worried she'd be able to smell what I'd done last night from across the room, I about catapulted myself out of the house.

The wind was a faint whisper of what it had been the night before, but I felt stronger, more sure. My friends were not bad people; I had to be able to talk some sense into them.

I rang Billie's doorbell at least ten times, before remembering it was Sunday morning, when, if her dad was feeling well, her family went out for breakfast. Man, I really was out of it these days. Singularly focused and not only ditching them, but forgetting the pattern of their lives. Okay, so maybe it would help if I started with an apology.

Wes then. He'd be the easy one anyway. The quickest entry point. He was, after all, the most reasonable.

A few blocks later, the warmth of the Thomas household wrapped itself around me. I didn't know if they actually kept the heat up, or if it was that Wes's mom always had something going in the kitchen. Wes's step-dad was wrestling with the three youngest on the living room floor in front of a football game, while his two older brothers shouted at the screen from the couch.

Wes hadn't said anything when he opened the door, but he moved to let me in, and I watched them all in the open space—living room to kitchen to dining area—while Wes slunk down the hall.

He most often got lost in it, being the slightest, most studious of the bunch.

His mom rushed over for a one-armed hug. "It's so nice to see you, Eden. I'm making chili for lunch if you want to stay." Then, patting me on the shoulder with her oven mitt, she made her way back across the chaos of the living room to the kitchen and her chili and her cornbread.

She put corn in her cornbread, and green onions and cheese. It was as warm as her house and as warm as her family.

But Wes was waiting for me, so I shuffled that way.

He'd moved down to the basement three years ago. His little brothers were triplets, an in vitro bunch resulting from his mom wanting babies with husband number two, and since it was a three-bedroom house—the master, the triplet's room, and one other—and since his older brothers had grown five inches each in high school, he said there was no longer room in there for him. He figured this would only last until they graduated and moved out, but they'd decided to stay home for college.

His space in the basement was huge, with a table and chairs he'd pulled in from the side of the curb, an old couch which had been down there before he claimed it, and an armchair Isaac gave him.

I sat in that chair, which still smelled like Isaac: bold and strong and slightly chlorinated. Though, the chair didn't always have a point to prove like Isaac did.

"Are we okay?" I asked. He hadn't said a word.

Wes looked up from his table, where his books were already sprawled out, as if he'd been up at six. "I don't know what we are."

"I'm sorry about what I said last night. And I'm sorry I've been kind of an awful friend lately."

"You've never been awful, Eden."

"Stop being so nice, Wes."

"Well, I'm not going to be mean."

"How many times have I ditched you?"

He went back to his homework. It was impressive he could have this conversation and do physics at the same time. "I stopped keeping track."

"Is that what last night was about?"

"What do you mean?"

"You guys didn't even give it a chance. You started in on me the moment you walked in."

"What did you expect?"

"That you'd make nice and get to know my new friends."

"Javi and Nat aren't new friends."

"Okay, so why haven't you ever gotten to know them?"

"They don't like us, remember?"

"They like me. Why would they not like you?" I stood and paced, frustrated that his face was still in his homework. "Is that what we do? We judge people because we think they don't like us? Of course they don't like us, if that's how we treat them." I stopped in front of him and he finally looked up. "Who cares, anyway, what others think, if we have each other?"

"That's a really good point, Eden."

See, he was the easy one. "You agree then? Is that what we've been doing?"

"Sure, maybe. But it doesn't matter, if we have each other."

We stared at each other a moment and I willed him to say he'd talk to Isaac. Maybe even Billie, because I'd probably soon be grounded. That he'd take care of things, and fix it, and join Hawk and Ivy for lunch, and we'd all be best friends. But that was me hiding behind him instead of hiding behind Billie.

Instead of saying all that, or doing it, he stood up and kissed me. Really planted his lips on mine and caught my waist when I was about to jump away. I yelped when his tongue got involved and shoved him back into his chair.

"That's not what I meant," I whispered.

He wouldn't look at me. "Shit."

"Please, Wes." I knelt down next to him and touched his elbow lightly. "Can't we just be friends? Can't things just be like they used to?"

He turned further away, his back curling a little, making me think of an armadillo—withdrawing into himself and putting up a shield. "I don't think you want anything to be how it used to. Isn't that the point?"

It was. He wasn't wrong. And yet somehow in those words I felt speared right through. "I'm so sorry, Wes."

"Just go, Eden."

"Wes."

"Please."

And then my mom was blowing up my phone.

18

GET YOUR ASS BACK HOME.

On my way, I replied. And suddenly I was awash in panic. Yes, I'd figured she'd kill me when she found out, but it had only been a guess, because I'd never been in trouble before.

Deep breaths, I instructed myself. She appreciated a sound, logical argument, so I mulled over my reasoning, trying to find one. It wasn't easy, and that brought me full circle back to the panic again.

She opened the front door before I made it up the walk, left it open, and retreated into the house.

Dropping my backpack on the front tile, I shut the door behind me and met her in the kitchen. Reese was nowhere to be found—probably in his room, maybe at a friend's house, definitely told to make himself scarce.

Sitting across from her, I rested my hands together on the table, letting my fingertips pull and push against the grain as I kept my head down and waited.

"I'm not exactly sure where to start here, Eden."

"I'm sorry, Mom."

"Sorry for what?"

"Sorry for drinking."

"That's it?"

I twisted my watch and searched for what else I might have done wrong.

"This new boy is bringing you to underage drinking parties. You're fighting with your friends who I know do not drink. You have a new friend I know nothing about, and she's behind these parties, hosting them at seventeen? Oh! And you can't handle your liquor responsibly. You wander out into the middle of a questionable neighborhood and throw up in the grass."

I raised an eyebrow. Well, that was nice of him, not telling her about the shoes. "Can I explain?"

"What's there to explain?"

None of it had seemed so terrible when it was happening, but when she put it that way, it sort of sounded like I'd been sneaking around, hanging with a bad crowd, and knowingly keeping it all from her—which, of course, implied guilt.

"Actually, I *would* like an explanation, Eden, if you have one." She closed her eyes and put a hand up between us. "No excuses, though, just information."

I spun my watch around my wrist. "Hawk is the boyfriend, and he's great, really, but it's only been a week and a half." I paused to let her respond, if she wanted to.

No. Okay.

"My friends... Wes likes me and even though he knows I'm with Hawk, he tried to kiss me, so you can imagine how awkward that makes things. I asked them to the party last night but they showed up kind of mean and judgmental without giving anyone a fair chance. So I'm kind of pissed at them and they're kind of pissed at me."

Still nothing.

"Ivy is Hawk's friend; she goes to our school and sings in a band. She lives with her cousin, who's also in the band, but her mom's okay with it. And she's sort of got fans and stuff, so a lot of the party was for the fans, you know? She's the one who gave me the magazines, but she's not what you think—she's great, too, and it's nice to have a friend who isn't Billie for once."

She frowned at that.

"I mean, Billie knows who she is and what she wants, and who I am and what I want, and I guess I wanted to try something else for a little while."

Her eyebrow jumped all over that. "Like drinking and parties?"

"Mom. I'm a senior in high school. How many kids my age do you think have never gone to a party or had a beer before?"

"You're not helping yourself right now."

I bit my tongue. Literally, I bit down on it, so as to not help myself anymore. But the tongue is the strongest muscle in the body, so they say, and it had more explaining it apparently wanted to do. "I wasn't in the middle of a questionable neighborhood alone. I'd been talking to Wes, and then Hawk was there too, and I could see the party, and there were a ton of people, and I was safe. I was more like, not alone in the middle of an apartment complex."

"Still not helping yourself."

I put my face in my hands. "I'm sorry," I mumbled. "Tell me what to do to make it up to you. Dishes for a week?"

"I'm not convinced you wouldn't make these same decisions all over again, Eden, and that's what worries me."

"I will never drink again, I promise. That, I agree, did not go so well. But I'm keeping my new friends."

She studied me. "I'm not sure I like the sound of this new friend."

"You can't tell me not to be friends with someone. I'm a little old for that."

"How did you meet this girl?"

"She's Hawk's best friend."

"Then I meet him first. And we talk about the girl later."

"Okay."

"Jerry said he seemed all right."

"He is all right. He's great."

"I always really liked Wes."

"I know. Me, too. Just not like that."

She nodded. "You're grounded for a week."

I blinked at her, opened my mouth, then closed it. It wasn't really a surprise, I guess, but I'd never been grounded before. I'd never even conceived that I'd be the type of girl to get grounded.

"I'd be happy not to see Ivy until then," I muttered. "If that's who you're trying to keep me from."

"No, Eden. I'm trying to keep you from yourself—Ivy? She's the singer?"

"Yes. You know, you might really like their shows. You and Jerry should come sometime—Thursdays and Saturdays at *The Sonic*—" I stopped myself there, before I dug my hole deeper.

"*The Sonic Boom* is a twenty-one-and-older club, Eden Rose Calloway. Would you like to be grounded another week for each time you've been to a club meant for *adults,* four years older than you?" She squinted at me a little. "Have you been missing volleyball practices, is that why your game has gotten worse?"

"Mom!"

"What? You want me to worry about hurting your feelings right now? It doesn't seem to me you care much about anything you used to, so volleyball probably doesn't matter either."

"It does!"

She crossed her arms. "It better. You need that for scholarships. You need something. You know I can't help you."

"I know! I know. I'm sorry, really. I'm just going through something right—"

"Oh, you are? You haven't mentioned it. Would you like to talk about it?"

I leaned back in my chair. "You're not too welcoming at the

moment."

She snapped her fingers at me. "Then no excuses! All you do for the next week is homework and think. Think about these choices you've been making and if they're really good for you, or if you've decided to start screwing up your life for the fun of it." She made some sort of *gah* noise and ran her hands over her face. "I count on you to help me set an example for Reese. He doesn't have a dad to look up to, to respect and listen to— he looks up to *you*. I don't know how I can keep him out of trouble on my own, when the exciting older sister is choosing the reckless stuff."

She pushed away from the table and went to the sink, placing her hands on the edge of it and staring out the window into our backyard. Grandpa's canoe was out there, upside down in the small flower garden my mom kept on her slower summers.

I sort of wanted to go crawl under it. Maybe she did, too.

I stood, but before I could walk out of the kitchen, she said, "Your phone. Your phone is mine because of that club business."

Monday

I saw Hawk before class and was able to tell him about the phone and grounding, but I wouldn't see Billie until third period. In second period study hall, I was busy formulating my sound, logical argument for her—after starting with a quick apology like I had with Wes, I'd go into all the reasons why she was being stupid at the party and should give Ivy and Hawk a chance—when I got called down to the office.

I didn't hear it at first. I mean, no one pays attention to the intercom, especially when you're not the type to get called down to the office. But the sophomore next to me whispered that they were calling my name, and then I heard it too: *Eden Calloway.*

Scrambling up, I slammed my knee on the underside of the table, nursed it for one second, then headed down the aisle.

Slowing, I wondered if I should grab my books. There was no one who'd grab them for me if I didn't make it back, and the sophomore was craning her neck to see what I'd been working on. I ran back and piled them up, gave her a look, and hustled past everyone who was not-so-thinly veiling their curiosity as to why goody-goody Eden Calloway was being called down to the office.

Hugging my books, I prayed it was nothing bad. The last time Mom had interrupted my school day was when Grandpa died. She'd been waiting in the office when I got there, standing blankly with one hand clasped to Reese's, who was white as a snow-washed winter day.

My feet were dragging with old worries and the possibility of new ones, but I didn't see her through the glass-paned wall as I turned the corner. Shuffling my books to one arm, I opened the door and walked up to the secretary.

"Excuse me, I was called down to the office?"

She looked up, her glasses tilted on her face.

"Eden Calloway?" I prodded.

"Ah, yes. Coach Warner wants to see you in his office."

"Oh!" Phew. Then it must be about the volleyball game tomorrow night. Maybe someone got hurt, maybe he was moving my position. Or maybe he was benching me because he agreed with my mom—that my game had been pathetic lately.

If I was benched, worst case scenario, I could still use volleyball as an extracurricular on college applications. I'd still be able to check that box, and the leadership box. Unless benched also meant he was taking the co-captain spot away from me. But I didn't think he'd do that, since we'd voted at the beginning of the year.

I wound my way through the depths of the school where the lockers gave way to solid cinder block, and knocked on the windowless door, which was propped open. He was scribbling at his desk, in the small room that still smelled like the mop buckets it used to closet, before the addition had been put on and he'd turned it into an office.

"Hi, Coach."

He glanced up. "Hi, Eden."

"What's up?" I asked.

Motioning to the only other chair in the room, he waited for me to sit, cleared his throat, and tented his fingertips together. "It's been brought to my attention that you've violated our athletic agreement."

"I'm sorry?"

"You are aware of our athletic agreement?"

I placed a hand to my cheek. I felt hot. Burning. I hadn't even thought of this worst-case scenario. "I am."

"You are aware of what you agreed to there?"

Isaac had gym first hour. That little bastard had gym first hour. Now I was choking, choking it out: "I am."

"What is it that you've agreed to, Eden?"

I couldn't believe he'd do this to me. Couldn't believe he'd turn me in. He was supposed to be my friend.

"To abstain from abusing alcohol or other recreational—

legal or illegal—drugs," he answered for me.

"I was absolutely not abusing, sir."

"Unfortunately, that's not the report I got."

"And you're going to believe it without hearing my side?"

"It comes from a very reputable source, but please, feel free to tell me your side. Were you *not* drinking on Saturday night?"

"I was, sir, but it was the first time *ever*. I didn't do anything stupid, nothing bad happened. Coach, please! Volleyball means everything to me—"

"It's up to my discretion, but the suggestion is that a tier-two violation should result in a suspension for thirty-five to seventy percent of the season. Seeing as this is your first offense, I'll rest on the light end, which will be five games."

"That's...is that the rest of the season?"

"Pretty much."

Horror flooded me, turning my hot cheeks to stone. "What about State?" We'd never win, we knew that. But getting there was half the battle. To not be part of it...

"You'd be back for Regionals. If State happens, you'll be with us. But as you'll be out of practice for three weeks, you won't be playing. You can come with the team and watch from the bench."

And then more horror, a gut-level dread that reached out over a lifetime. "But this could ruin my scholarship chances." Would I have to lie on those applications? I couldn't do that. "I need those, please, sir. Please don't do this." Placing a fist in one eye socket, I willed myself not to lose it here. Not at school. Not in front of a teacher I respected. Not when I had to be the mature, responsible adult who wouldn't abuse alcohol or other recreational—legal or illegal—drugs.

His face softened. "Actions have consequences, Eden, and you knew what those would be. I'm sorry."

"There's nothing I can do? You said it was up to your discretion."

"Not at this time." His tone was a kind of cold fatigue. "Go home and talk to your mom about it. If she wants to call and plead your case… No, you should probably plead your own case. I don't know. Let's both think about it for a bit, okay?"

I nodded. I nodded the burning away, and I nodded until I could walk out of there without bursting into tears.

One night. One time. One bad decision that millions of other kids have made, and I'm the one who got caught. I'm the one whose mother's boyfriend has to live in the same apartment building. The one whose friend thinks there's nothing more important than telling the truth.

No matter the consequences.

20

It took a while to pull it together after my talk with Coach Warner. All I kept thinking was *not at this time.* Which wasn't a no, but then he'd left me with nothing, not even a place to start.

Hawk swung by with the hive of students as they swarmed the hall. I stared blankly at him, and when he asked if something was wrong, I told him I couldn't talk about it right now. I was afraid if I did, I would burst into tears.

People went blurry, buzzing by in streaks of color, because my eyes were filling again. I turned around, switched my books out of my locker, and rested my head against the inside of the door, on a picture of Billie and me, until the noise behind me died down.

I had nothing to say to her anymore. How could she have let him do this?

Like a zombie, that's how I made it through third period. Listless and devoid of care.

As we filed out, she sighed heavily. "You're being quite dramatic, you know?"

I opened my mouth but no noise made it out. How could I tell her what was happening, how could I explain what type of girl I'd become, how could I admit I was going to lose it on Isaac? Nope, it would just have to play out at lunch, and she could catch up. Because I couldn't start crying about volleyball and my college applications and scholarships and my future before I confronted him. I needed anger and righteousness on my side.

I forced my legs to our lunch table, which, come to think of it, I hadn't been at for a while.

Billie sat down with her brown bag next to Isaac, and Wes sat across from them with his lunch tray. Centered between them, as if he'd gotten used to taking up both of our spots while I'd been gone. When he saw me coming, he ducked his head and shoved food faster into his mouth. As if he were saying *Nope, lips busy. Don't worry, I won't try that again.*

Unless *he'd* turned me in, because of the kiss. But he didn't have gym first hour.

I planted my palms on the table and glared at Isaac. "Seriously?" The word came out like gunfire. "I thought we were supposed to be friends."

The fork stalled on its way to his mouth. "Huh?"

"I know you think you know everything and what's best for everyone, blah, blah, blah, but I didn't think you'd ever screw me over like this."

"Eden, I don't know what you're talking about."

I tried to gauge how good he could be at lying, after having never done it in his entire life, but who else could it have been? Wes was looking at me now, curious. If it had been him, he wouldn't be so innocent. And not only did Isaac have gym first period, but he'd essentially said as much to Javi and Nat at the party.

"Coach Warner," I snapped.

"Shit, Eden," Wes choked on his fry a bit. "Did you get kicked off the team?"

Isaac's eyes widened to match Wes's and I nodded. They stared at me like I was someone they didn't know. Someone who was shifty enough to get kicked off a team. They didn't rub elbows with people like that.

We, previously, hadn't rubbed elbows with anyone like that.

"I will never forgive you for this."

"I didn't do it!"

"Want me to tell your swim coach you were there, too?"

"Eden!" he cried. "I swear, I didn't do it!"

But of course he would say that to keep himself clean. He'd do anything to keep himself clean. Even lie. "Who else could it have possibly been?"

"Hawk?" Billie asked, as a hand slid across my back and curved along my side.

"Hawk what?" he asked from behind me.

"Turned her in, to Coach Warner."

"Who's Coach Warner?"

"Our PE instructor," Billie informed him, a clip to her voice conveying what she thought about a person who never showed up for gym.

"Her volleyball coach," Wes added.

"Turned you in for what?" Hawk asked.

"The party and the out-of-character drinking," Isaac stated, like a mom might.

I flung back to him. "See! Of *course* you did it!"

"Maybe Hawk wants you free to keep making bad decisions," Billie whispered, as if he wouldn't hear it. "Or maybe he just wants you all to himself.

Hawk's hand dropped from my side. "I what?"

"Oh, now he's a controlling stalker boyfriend? I cannot believe you." I stood up straight, every vertebra tense. "This is all me, Billie. All these decisions I'm making, just because they're not yours, doesn't mean they can't be mine. I wanted to go to that party. I wanted to drink. So sorry that for once I wanted to do something you didn't. Sorry I wanted to be someone you aren't."

"Doesn't sound like Warner is all that off base, then." Isaac pointed a fry at me, which I snatched out of his hand, squeezed into a pulp, and threw back onto his tray.

"I will *never* forgive you," I told him. Then to Billie: "How could you let him do this? You know how important college is to me, how bad I need those scholarships. I was counting on volleyball and being a co-captain, and you knew that."

She straightened her shoulders and her face. "If Isaac says he didn't do it, I believe him."

Trying not to sputter as I pulled in all the air that would deliver what I wanted to say to my shitty, judgmental, backstabbing best friends, I opened my mouth to let it loose, but Hawk pulled me away.

"Come on," he soothed. "Don't make it worse."

"How could I make it worse? He totally screwed me! And for what? Because he wants me with Wes?! I thought maybe, just maybe, I mattered more to him than that."

"Maybe he's protecting Billie," Hawk said.

He'd gotten me outside, where the scent of fresh clove wafted by. I recoiled from it and stumbled away from the seniors who didn't care if we weren't supposed to smoke on school property. "You mean you think *she* did it?" No, I couldn't believe that.

He followed me, put his hands on my arms, and turned me toward him. "No, I mean maybe he did it because of what went down this weekend. To defend her. To help get you back on track—to her."

Or to defend Wes. I forced my shoulders to relax. "I should tell you that Wes kissed me yesterday. I'm sorry, I forgot this morning, after talking to my mom, but it meant nothing, obviously. I shoved him away, and—"

He pulled me against him and brushed the hair over my shoulder to place his face there, his mouth near my ear. "All you had to say was it meant nothing."

Or had it meant everything? Was that what caused all this? But it was so unlike Wes to force anything. He was the one I could count on to *not* do that. Not that I could count on him for anything anymore. Not that I could count on any of them.

I'd been uprooted, this new me. Firmly and thoroughly. No more ties to old Eden.

21

The house was quiet that afternoon, after I told my mom and brother I wouldn't be at volleyball the next day, or the day after that, or the day after that.

My mom didn't seem to give me any points for telling her, when I could have used it as my one window of freedom. And Reese was clearly disappointed with me, appalled that I'd quit. Mom had given me a look, but I wasn't sure what she wanted me to do—be the good example who wouldn't have done anything to be kicked off the team, or be the good example who took responsibility for herself and didn't lie.

I settled for telling Reese it was more complicated than that, promising him, and myself, that it wouldn't last forever.

When he walked by my room later, instead of stopping by to see what I was doing and tell me about his day, he studied the faded hardwood floor. I walked into the hall, but Reese went to his room and closed the door firmly behind him. Alarming how someone could feel so let down when they didn't even know the half of it.

My mom appeared at the end of the hall, a question on her face. With a shrug, I turned, closing my door too.

She opened it when dinner was ready. I said I wasn't hungry and she disappeared without seeming to care. But then

Jerry appeared with a plate and set it on my nightstand. I was on my bed, surrounded by a haphazard array of open books.

"I wanted to apologize," he said, after stopping for a moment by the quotes I'd hung. "For telling your mom about the party."

"But you'd do it again."

"I would, but even so, I hope it's not too terrible for you."

When I didn't reply, he nodded and moved toward the door. Before walking out, he turned back. "My favorite has always been: *Sometimes we're tested. Not to show our weaknesses, but to discover our strengths.*"

That was a good one. And he'd brought me dinner. And he was doing right by my mom. I couldn't be too mad at him.

After he'd gone, a light knuckle rapped against my window. Hawk. Checking that my door was closed—locked, I turned on some music and opened it.

"You have to come in," I whispered. "In case Jerry sees you when he leaves." If only my window looked out on the backyard instead of the side.

I offered him a hand but he didn't take it, and it was reasonably comical watching him climb inside. I grinned from my bed as he rested on the window seat to catch his breath. "Not very coordinated, are we?"

Meeting and matching my smirk, he charged, tumbling into me so we fell flat on my mattress, me on my back and him next to me on his stomach. After extricating a few books from beneath us, I turned so I could see his face.

"I didn't know you were coming," I said.

"Well, it's not like I could text you." He propped himself up next to me. "Your mom's replying to everyone, very nicely, that you're grounded, phoneless, and all interactions will need to be limited to school hours."

"Who's everyone?"

"Me, Ivy, Javi—she's in English with me. We're buddies now." He slid his fingers through mine and held our hands up between us, watching them and not me. "I don't know if it's true or not," he said, "but Ivy told me that in French, you don't say *I miss you*, but something more like *You are missing from me.*"

I smiled. "I like that."

His attention moved from our hands to my face. "I like *you.*"

"I like you, too," I whispered.

"I don't want to get you in trouble."

"My door's locked."

"Your window's not."

I thought for a moment that perhaps I should drop my curtains, so it was harder to see in, but I didn't want to move— our bodies were in perfect alignment. Nose to nose, hand on hand, knees to knees, calves and feet hanging off the bed. I was afraid if I got up, I wouldn't be able to come back and replicate this, and I wasn't ready to give it up yet.

"I just wanted to share more of your poem, then I'll go."

"Okay."

"Okay, but I'm going to start from the beginning this time." He cleared his throat, then closed his eyes and rested his forehead against mine. *"The warmth of your hair would calm a bitter night. The depth of your eyes set a hurricane right. The scent of your skin, your hand gripped in mine—we dissolve darkness; catch, link, and entwine. To reach out for nothing and come back with you; please tell me, tell me, it's all true—"*

It was beautiful, but I really wanted him to open his eyes. I couldn't know he was seeing me if he wasn't even looking. I couldn't know it was really me he was talking to or thinking about.

"You're not an illusion, a joke that's been played, and you won't leave me here open and flayed. You've found pieces of me, essentials I need. So say the words, whisper them, scream..."

I waited as his voice drifted off, but his eyes stayed shut. Squeezed shut now, actually, like he was unsure of himself, afraid my reaction wasn't going to be what he wanted it to be. And maybe it wouldn't, because two weeks was too soon for I-love-yous. But there was so much between us anyway, in such a short amount of time. Gathering his t-shirt in my fist, I tried to make sense of all that.

"It feels like I've been waiting for you forever," I whispered, when he opened his eyes. "You know how when you like someone, even though you maybe don't know them, you like them and like them and like them, and then you get to know them and they're everything you thought they'd be, plus more? And you know you shouldn't jump in so fast, but it feels like you're just catching up to the scenarios your mind has been playing out in your head for so long. It's confusing, because you don't want to miss all the lovely beginnings, but you can't help speeding through to the place your heart is waiting."

I bit my lips to stop the outpouring, not knowing where it came from. It did help explain how I so badly wanted to jump him right now, this boy in my bed, when the most I'd had before were his kisses, and the friendly advances of Wes.

His lips offered up the brightest, widest smile I'd seen from him yet, which positively lit up his face. "You liked me and liked me and liked me?"

I nodded, slowly.

"You can be quite poetic yourself."

"Hardly."

"Don't underestimate yourself, Eden. You're euphonious and I hear you. I *hear* you."

That was all it took for us to be on each other, fast and bold and needy. And the door swung open before I had time to register the click of it being unlocked with a skeleton key.

Hawk froze, my heart stopped, and my mom loomed as large as I'd ever seen her in the doorway. Her gaze flittered to the window, gaping open without the screen, and her hands went to her hips, making her loom even larger.

"Have you been sneaking out, too?!" she cried.

"No!" I scrambled off the bed. "No! No, I promise!"

Hawk jumped up and reached a hand out to her, as if she were in any mood to shake it in greeting. "This is the first time I've been in, Ma'am. I swear. And it was only to make sure Eden was okay after the volleyball fiasco."

"This is not how I'd hoped to meet you, Hawk." She spit his name out as if he were an actual predatory bird picking at the bones of her dead daughter.

I stepped in front of him, pushing his hand back to his side and holding him behind me. "This is not his fault."

"You are now grounded another two weeks." She stalked over to my window, shut it, locked it, and piled books from my nearby bookshelf in front of it.

Jerry slipped into the room and took her hands in his, which seemed to calm her a bit, while Hawk and I watched from the middle of the room. Reese stood in the doorway, and when I noticed him, my heart sank lower, if it even could.

Reese disappeared, and Hawk stepped around me. "I'm sorry we met like this, Ms. Calloway. I hope we can do it right next time." Before she could answer, he slipped from the room and found his way out.

My mom speared me with what felt like a final look, then instructed Jerry to please take my bedroom door off.

Tuesday

"I wanted to text you last night," I admitted to Billie in third period the next day.

"Why didn't you?" she asked, from a distance. There was now distance between us.

"I no longer have my phone. Didn't I tell you I was grounded?"

She shot me a look.

"I threw up on Jerry's shoes on Saturday after you guys left. He told my mom I was at a raging party and sloppy drunk."

"You weren't sloppy drunk."

"Thank you."

During class, I thought about all the things I wanted to say to her, about how awful they'd been at the party and how she still hadn't apologized. It seemed to trump everything that had happened before it, back when I'd been the one who owed them an apology, but all that tempered my anger a bit.

When the bell rang, I'd decided to go with: "So, about the party."

She only raised an eyebrow. I'd been hoping she'd take that sentence and run with it for me, do the heavy lifting. When she didn't, I swept up my books. "I'm sorry I've ditched you guys so much lately."

Cue her apology. Only, she just kept walking.

"I was trying to bring everyone together, you know?"

She stopped in the hall, so I stopped with her. "You knew we weren't going to drink."

"Fine, so don't drink. But give it a chance."

"You pretty much shoved beer in our faces the minute we got there."

"I asked if you wanted one. You didn't. I moved on. Then you told me I looked like a whore, and Wes called my boyfriend a loser."

She glanced into the masses as they stormed toward lunch, or fourth period, whichever way their schedule leaned. Her pursed lips meant she was speechless or pained, but I was going to believe either meant my point had hit home.

"They're good people, Billie. You can't not give them a chance just because you think they're not going to like you."

"I don't care if they like me, Eden. That's the thing. And you shouldn't either."

"What, I should only care if you like me?" Because that was the problem here, wasn't it? Her friendship, apparently, was conditional.

"We're trying to look out for you."

"I put on some makeup, borrowed a shirt, and tested out what alcohol felt like. Don't worry, I'm not planning on doing any of that again. So was one night really worth throwing me under the bus?"

"It's not one night, Eden. We can't even tell who you are anymore."

"How about supporting me then, instead of judging me?"

"We would, if you'd let us."

"On your terms. If I have no other friends."

She rolled her eyes. "Stop being so dramatic."

"Just, never mind," I muttered.

"Fine. I will never mind." And off she went, just like that.

I stood in the hall a minute, letting the current rush around me until it slowed and cleared, a thick ball of cotton growing in my throat.

"EDEN CALLOWAY!" Javi's voice boomed from across the hall.

Nat slid up to me first. "Why weren't you at practice last night?"

As usual, though, they didn't really wait for me to answer. "Coach was all vague about you not being there."

"Awesome party."

"You actually threw up on your mom's boyfriend?"

"How'd that happen?"

"What was he even doing there?"

The three of us started walking toward the parking lot where I was supposed to meet Hawk and Ivy. "He lives there, I guess. And I'm suspended. That's why I wasn't at practice."

Javi stopped in her tracks. "I'm sorry, what?"

"Because of the athletic agreement."

"Someone turned you in?"

I nodded.

"How many games?" Javi asked.

"Pretty much all of them."

"Fuck!" she shouted. Then, at regular volume again, "What about State? He can't do that to us."

Nat grabbed her arm. "This is about Eden, Javs. She doesn't deserve this." They stared at each other, imagining, maybe, how they deserved it more than I did. Yeah. Same.

Javi puffed out a few quick breaths. "Okay, trying not to freak out here. There has to be a way to get you back on the team."

I walked to the end of the hall and turned to face them, back pressed against the door. "I don't know, but I'll figure it out if there is, okay?"

"Okay." Javi nodded like a bobblehead. "Okay."

"Let us know if you need anything."

I nodded and left, because I couldn't think about it anymore than I already had. I'd been up half the night wondering if an essay would do, or some huge show of devotion like serenading the team, but everything I'd thought of was that stupid or worse.

Ivy was already in the front seat of Hawk's car, which wasn't much of a surprise. Hawk called it for me every day, but if she got there first, she took it. I slid into the back and buckled myself in.

She twisted in the seat. "Why so sad, lovey?"

"My life has fallen apart."

"Your old life," she corrected. "Your new life is sitting in this car with you."

"Ivy," Hawk muttered, backing out of his parking spot.

"What? Who needs 'em?"

"Most people do not have such an easy time writing people off," he replied.

"Who have I written off?" she asked. "You and I have been soul mates for ten years."

"Where are we going?" I asked as Hawk passed the last of our usual lunch spots, carefully ignoring the *soul mates* bit.

"Ivy thinks she's going to cheer you up."

"I am going to cheer you up."

"We're not skipping class, right? Because that would not help me right now."

Hawk caught my eye in the rear-view. "No, I don't need to dig myself a deeper hole with your mother."

"Hey! Speaking of your mother." Ivy turned around again. "I met her boyfriend the other day. He's cute, huh?"

I rested back against the seat with a snort. "I've never really thought about it."

"Really? Because that ass..." she trailed off as Hawk cleared his throat and I made a face.

"I have never and will never assess his ass."

"I would highly recommend it." She winked.

"Back up," Hawk said. "How'd this happen?"

"He was bringing in groceries as I was coming out of the apartment. Said he thought I was a friend of his girlfriend's daughter." She pointed over her shoulder at me. "Said she was at a party the other night, *Eden Calloway?* I nodded and he shook my hand, said it was nice to meet me. That's it. Then he walked away and I enjoyed the view."

I groaned. "My mom must have told him to keep an eye on your place."

Hawk pulled into a huge, empty parking lot where an office building stood in the distance, dark and deserted.

I scooted up and over to him, resting my arms on the back of his seat and my head near his. "What are we doing?"

Ivy got out and marched around to the driver's side, opened Hawk's door, and motioned for him to vacate the seat. He joined me in back. Ivy slid in, locked all the doors, and turned to me, stage face on. "When I'm pissy, all it takes is a little speed and a few tight circles." Then she put her foot to the pedal so fast I was left scrambling for my seatbelt.

Hawk simply braced himself, legs and arms splayed out in

every direction. On the first donut she pulled, my brain rocked in its skull.

On the second, my stomach rolled. "Oh, please stop," I muttered.

"I think she's gonna be sick," Hawk warned, right before Ivy slammed on the brakes.

I stumbled out of the car. Ivy and Hawk both met me behind it. Hawk put a hand on my back as I doubled over and gasped for air, hoping I wouldn't ralph right there in front of them.

"Your turn," Ivy said. "You won't get sick if you're driving."

"I don't want to."

"Yes, you do." She swept her arm around the lot, peppered with nothing but a handful of light posts. "There's nothing for you to hurt here, and you need the release. Trust me." She grabbed my hand and put me behind the wheel, then slid in the front passenger seat and cranked the music up as loud as it would go.

I held my hands to my ears with a whimper.

Reaching between us from the back seat, Hawk turned the music off. "You don't have to do this."

But when I didn't, Ivy straddled the cup holders to put her foot down on the gas pedal. I screamed bloody murder as the car shot forward. My foot, in panic, went for the brake. She was laughing, holding onto me, jamming her foot as far as it would go. The car roared while both the gas and brake were pressed, until Hawk shoved Ivy back into her seat.

She was beaming, eyes bright. "See?" she cried. "Don't you feel better?"

Hawk looked unconcerned. But this was his *soul mate*, after all.

I, on the other hand, couldn't move. I felt like the car was going to take off of its own accord, most likely when I was half in and half out. Hawk got out, pulled open my door, and offered me a hand.

"Wait!" Ivy said. "She didn't do any circles! Eden, you have to do a circle."

"I am not doing a circle." I would do anything in this whole world to avoid it. "In fact, I think I might walk back."

"Then you'll be skipping class," Hawk pointed out.

I removed my shaking hands from the wheel, and he helped me out of the car. Wrapping me up, he rested his face against my neck. His steady breathing anchored me to the ground. I closed my eyes and breathed with him until it reset my coordinates.

When he pulled away, he had that smile on his face that made my stomach burn, and he whispered. "Sorry, I told her you wouldn't like it, but..." *But Ivy gets what she wants.*

"It's okay." I pulled my hand from his and put a finger to his lips. "Let's never talk of it again."

Ivy honked the horn and I about jumped out of my skin. Not completely recalibrated then. I took a deep breath and Hawk leaned into the car. "Get in the back, Ivy, or Eden's not getting in."

She huffed, but complied, and as we drove back to the school, her feet hung out the window behind me.

"Is this because I didn't text you back last night?" I asked.

"Of course not, silly. Your mom and I had a nice little chat." She beamed at me. "We're chatting."

"You're chatting?"

"Yep, don't worry. I got this."

Leaning back in the seat, I closed my eyes. I couldn't deal with that right now. I just couldn't. I'd worry about my stomach, and my soupy brain. The rest I'd have to think about later.

A few days later...

Life without volleyball, friends, and a phone gave me too much time to think. So much that I'd go from convincing myself everything was my fault, to wondering what I'd done that was so bad and back again.

No doubt I wouldn't have made the same choices before Hawk and Ivy, so I could see why my mom might have an issue there. The old me would have tagged my recent decisions as horrible before making them.

Tag and delete.

"Eden?" Reese looked up from his homework.

I was putting dinner together. BLTs. That's what a girl did when she had no volleyball, no friends, and no phone.

"Need some help?" I asked, grabbing for the towel and wiping the traces of tomato off my hands.

He shook his head and put his math packet back in his folder.

"What's up?"

"What did you do to make Mom so mad?"

"It doesn't matter. We're good now." I motioned behind me. "Look, I'm even making her dinner."

"You're grounded, though."

I nodded. But Mom wanted me to set a good example, so I wasn't going to tell him why. It was the least I could do for her, at this point.

"Was it because of that boy?"

"That I'm grounded?"

He nodded.

Sliding into the seat across from him, I shook my head. "It had nothing to do with him. I made my own choices. And the thing is, not every choice seems bad at the time, okay? The important thing is that when you realize it was a bad choice, you take responsibility and do your best to make it right. You do your time and make dinner and get back on track."

But I wasn't getting back on track. If you looked at it from his perspective, I'd lost everything. My life had consisted of Billie, Wes, Isaac, volleyball, and school. All that was left of that was school, and I'd even been putting off my stupid psych paper.

"But you didn't make bad decisions before," my brother said, this time a little quieter.

"Before what?"

"Before that boy."

It prickled me, this sentiment suggesting Hawk was bad and had rubbed off on me. "That's not fair, Reese, to call someone good or bad before you know them."

"But you know him, right?"

"Some people will be different from you, or taught different things. Some have different expectations set on them—or no expectations—and they live life in a different way, but that doesn't mean they're wrong or bad. Got it?"

He shrunk a little, but nodded. "So he's different but not bad?"

I sighed, not quite grasping why this was so important. "He's kind and gentle and sweet. He writes poetry and helps his mom. In my book, that's all very good."

"Do you think Jerry is good?"

Ah. With a smile, I stood to check on the bacon. "I think Jerry is much more like us than Hawk. Don't worry about him."

"Then you don't think Mom will start making bad choices now, too?"

"I promise you she won't." I looked back at him. "But you're in charge of yourself, okay? You're in charge of your own choices. I don't want to hear you trying to blame anyone else, ever."

I waited for his nod before turning back to dinner, but the conversation stayed with me. I was in charge of myself, and the choices I'd made lately had lost me everything I'd cared about. I might have been a newish person since that Wednesday two weeks ago, but that didn't mean I didn't still care about those same things. And if that were true, then I probably wasn't all that much different than I'd always been, so what the hell did it all mean anyway?

Grabbing the lettuce from the fridge, I slammed the door out of frustration.

Reese's soft voice floated over from the table. "Are you mad at me?" He'd packed up his homework and was standing there with his bad slung over his back.

I motioned for a hug. When he didn't come, I dropped my arms. "Of course not. I'm mad at me. But I'll get it figured out. I promise."

He stared at me a moment, then nodded and headed to his room.

Saturday

Since I was now reluctant to get in a car with Ivy, the three of us spent two weeks of lunches on the grass, enjoying the cool weather before the cold swooped in. Mostly, Hawk and Ivy rehashed what they'd done the night before.

For two weeks, I'd bit my tongue from asking where Tony had been, as he'd shown up maybe twice in their stories. It didn't matter. I refused to be the jealous girlfriend, no matter how close Ivy sat to Hawk, or how often she touched him, or how far she leaned over his lap when she got laughing hard enough.

What mattered was that I had my phone back, and Jerry had convinced my mom to go to *The Sonic Boom* for Ivy's show. Ivy invited her via their new text friendship via my phone, and this meant I got to go, too.

The first thing I did was look at their conversation. It felt like snooping, but how could it be when it was my phone? Ivy had started by telling my mom what a good influence I was, what an 'upstanding human' she'd raised. Then my mom grilled her about her life, Ivy answering with loads of charm, and the last text was Ivy asking her if she wanted to come see her perform. My mom hadn't answered, but now we were going.

"Are Billie and Wes coming?" my mom asked as I paced the living room.

I stopped and stared. She'd curled her hair into loose waves, swept them over to one side with a bobby pin, and was actually wearing lipstick you could see, as opposed to the neutral shade she wore to work. Her flowy tank top, dark skinny jeans, and black booties were even fairly cool. If she had a sleek leather jacket instead of a sweater, I might have sworn I'd seen her at the club before.

She did her hair and makeup for work, but this wasn't the same. This was a third persona—from mom to paralegal to woman-on-a-date—and it struck me that a person could be three things at once. Just like Nat and Javi when they'd shown up to that party looking so different from how they dressed for school. Duh, I guess. A person didn't have to be all one thing or the other; they could be a little of both.

"Eden. Are Billie and Wes coming?"

I started pacing again. Jerry and Reese had gone out to pick up Chinese food, and Hawk would be here any minute. "Billie and Wes wouldn't be caught dead within a twenty-mile radius of any place that serves alcohol."

She gave me one of her colossal frowns like I was being rude about my friends, but at this point, I think that was pretty safe to say.

The doorbell rang and I sprang toward it, flinging the door open like some dramatic movie moment. Hawk was running one hand through his hair, while the other held a cute succulent in a small, geometric pot.

"Hi," I breathed.

"Hey," he breathed back.

Yep. We were on the same nervous page.

"Come in, Hawk," my mom said from behind me.

"Of course, Ma'am. This is for you." And he handed her the plant.

She raised an eyebrow. "That's very thoughtful. Thank you."

He nodded. "My mom prefers these to flowers because she appreciates their self-sufficiency. This echeveria has always been my favorite."

She raised both eyebrows. "You know your succulents."

"Plants in general, actually. Some kids are obsessed with trains; I was obsessed with gardens. Don't ask me why." He laughed a little, but it was unlike any laugh I'd ever heard from him. I slipped my hand through his, and we followed my mom as she walked the pot into the kitchen and set it on the windowsill over the sink.

"I'm a little obsessed with plants too. Did Eden tell you?"

We both shook our heads.

"I've been thinking of doing a little rock garden out on the corner this summer."

"Let me know if you want any help. I always liked to dig, too."

We stared at each other for a few moments before Reese came charging through the front door. "Jerry got extra fortune cookies! Mom! Mom! We got extra fortune cookies!"

He dumped an armful down on the kitchen table and stood back to admire them.

I laughed, my mom ruffled his hair, and Jerry came in with a smile on his face. "Easy to please, that one. Hello, Hawk."

"Hi, sir."

"Please, call me Jerry. Unless you want me calling you son."

Hawk nodded. "Duly noted."

"So, Hawk." My mom sat down at the table while Jerry opened the boxes and set them on the table. "How many windows have you snuck through in your life?"

He blanched and I choked, the subsequent coughing causing Hawk to pat me on my back.

"Mom!" I cried, once I'd recovered.

"Three?" he answered.

We both looked at him, then she turned to me. "You can't expect me to brush that under the rug."

"It was my fault. He was just checking on me and I made him come in."

"Well, he snuck into my house. So he can tell me about the three times and then I'll consider the issue resolved."

Oh, but if only he didn't have to do it in the face of that frown. Reese was looking at the tabletop, and Jerry had his back to us at the counter, dishing dinner onto plates.

Hawk cleared his throat. "One time, in elementary school, I snuck out my bedroom window when my mom and brother were fighting. I'd just learned how to put the screens in and take them out. In middle school, I snuck out for a concert, but only because I didn't want my mom to worry if I was out all night, not because she said no or wouldn't have let me go. She probably would've. I've never really had reason to sneak."

"Until recently."

"Well, I knew she was grounded, Ma'am. I really just wanted to check on her because of the volleyball thing."

"That was the first time you'd been at her window?"

"The second? But it was the first time I snuck in."

"Why not come to the door in the first place?"

"It's not nearly as romantic."

"I don't want you coming to her window."

"Of course, Ma'am."

"You'll have to find another way to be romantic."

"I do write poetry."

She motioned to the table, for him to take a seat, breaking what felt to be a standoff of sorts. Reese unfroze himself and started sorting the fortune cookies into five piles, and Jerry brought the plates to the table.

"Is that what you plan to do with your future?" she asked, more conversationally this time. Though asking someone if they wanted to be an artist the rest of their life did seem to be another test.

"I mean, that'd be amazing, but I'm not going to bank on it." He chose a seat next to her, which had to have been a strategic move. "I'd love to be a school counselor, but that requires a master's, and to be honest, I'm not sure that's in the cards for me. I'll probably start as a paramedic and maybe try to get a bachelor's down the road for social work. See what happens."

I looked at him in surprise. He'd never told me that.

He very slightly raised an eyebrow in return, as if to say I'd never asked.

"I've thought about being a school counselor, too" I admitted.

"Do you play piano?" Reese asked, as I slowly went back to my larger-than-average pile of potstickers.

"I do, actually." Hawk smiled at him. "Just a bit."

"Me, too!" Reese grinned back. "Wes doesn't."

I coughed a little, but Hawk didn't miss a beat. "Well, I bet you could teach me a few things, just like you could teach Wes."

"He only plays chopsticks. He says that's all he's got in him."

"Do you know *Heart and Soul*?"

"Yes! Everyone knows that."

Hawk leaned forward. "Let's do it after dinner."

"After the fortune cookies."

"Right."

"A poet," Jerry said, with a slow nod. "And music. Books or sports, then?"

"Books, for sure. And yes, all the music."

They launched into a conversation about a million bands I'd never heard of, and I finished my lo mein, egg fried rice, and sesame chicken. It was easier to eat when it was easier to breathe.

~

It was a little different, and definitely less anxiety-inducing, walking in the front door of a bar with my mom. Where she went, I could legally go, too. Hawk commandeered a table, and as soon as we were settled, my mom asked that I go get her a beer.

"What?"

"I want to know if they'll serve you. Wait, do you have a fake? Wallets, please." She put her hand out and motioned to both me and Hawk. He slid his over without missing a beat. She eyeballed me. "Wallet, Eden Rose."

I gritted my teeth—though I had no fake—and yanked it out of my purse.

She flipped open to Hawk's driver's license as Jerry flung an arm around her shoulder, and it occurred to me that I was on a double date with my mother. Rifling through my wallet more thoroughly than she had Hawk's, she gave them back and I stood, thankful she hadn't requested Hawk prove anything, since the bartender served him without question.

With hands flapping at my sides, I did my best to be smooth while approaching the bar. I had never actually approached a bar, and I wasn't sure if I was supposed to hail the bartender like you hailed a cab, or if that would be ridiculous.

To be safe, I waited until he glanced at me, then raised my eyebrows like I might want something.

He raised them back, finished what he was doing, then came over and placed his hands on the wooden ledge.

"Can I help you?"

"I'd like a beer, please."

"You would, huh?"

"Right, whatever you have."

"You got ID?"

"Not on me."

"Then you're out of luck."

"Excellent, thank you!" I grinned, too large, and made my way back to my mom. "He asked for an ID," I reported. "Wouldn't serve me without one."

She settled back in her chair. "Jerry, would you get me a Moscow Mule?"

"What's that?" I asked, leaning into the table.

"It's an alcoholic beverage. And that's two points for you

not knowing."

I scoffed. "Since when do you drink?"

"Since when did I stop drinking?" she countered, as Jerry scooted his chair back and got up. "I just do so responsibly."

Ivy, Jay, Tony, and the bass guitar guy took the stage. The crowd erupted, and Ivy hopped to her microphone with a big smile and a loud welcome.

That was pretty much the last I watched her, though, as my attention was on my mother the entire time. She had to like it. She just had to.

Jerry was cheering with the crowd in no time, and he wasn't even drinking. Apparently, he used to frequent this local circuit too—something their indie band dinner conversation had revealed. My mom was smiling at Hawk, a lot, which I took to mean she'd officially and completely forgiven him for the making-out-with-me-in-my-locked-bedroom-on-my-actual-bed-after-sneaking-in-through-the-busted-window-when-I-was-grounded thing.

It was perfect. My mom was having fun, I'd passed the drinking-at-a-bar test, and she'd meet Ivy after the show, when Ivy was at her most mesmerizing.

Things were finally weaving themselves back together. If I could get my mom on board with an over twenty-one club, then there had to be a way back onto the volleyball team.

I relaxed into the slower-than-average chords coming from the stage, my attention going there fully when the words oozing out of Ivy's mouth rang oddly familiar. And not because I'd heard her sing the song before.

> "...I reach in the darkness,
> not sure what I'll grasp,
> not sure it's for nothing,
> until your hand is in mine,
> raising me from darkness,
> and twining us, vines.
> Oooooh, baby, please tell me you are true..."

My throat tightened and my heartbeat thumped with the staccato of the last line. She'd punched the words out and each was a hit to my ego. It felt like a secret between Hawk and I had been bared for all the world to see. Like she'd taken a nude photo of our relationship and plastered it everywhere for people to see.

I turned on Hawk, but he was as caught up as every other drooling male in the place. Mouth slightly open, attention transfixed on Ivy swaying with the languidly sexy beat.

"Tell me that you're true, I need to know you're true, I want you to be truuuuuuuue. . ."

Again and again, she repeated his words, the verse of a poem he'd supposedly written for me. A poem he hadn't finished yet. Unless he had. Unless he'd finished it for someone else. Unless he'd written it for her and used it on me because it sounded good, because he knew I'd fall for it.

"Oooooh, baby, please tell me that you're true,
that you're not some illusion,
or a joke that's been played,
And you won't—please don't—
leave me open and flayed.
In you I've found pieces,
essentials I need.
So say the words,
whisper them, screeeeeeeeeeam."

Then she began to chant, *"Whisper them, scream, tell me, tell me, whisper them scream."* This was all he'd shared with me so far. Whatever came next was new. I pulled my hand away from his and he turned to me, shaking his head. Then it came:

"There's no choice any longer,
I'm here to staaaaaaay.
You're my hope, my desire,
Lead me awaaaaay."

As she went into more chanting, the bile rose in my throat. Who, exactly, was his hope and desire, if he'd shared it with her first?

She'd made sure I knew how close they were—soul mates, even. She hung all over him, all the time, and hardly gave us any chance to be alone.

I stood so abruptly that my chair tumbled back on the floor.

So much for my mother meeting Ivy. So much for things working out.

I rushed through the bar and out the front door for air, but it didn't slam right away, and then Hawk was there, reaching for my hand.

Yanking my arm back into my chest, I spun away from him, into the dirty brick wall, bracing my side against it.

"Eden. Eden, listen. It's supposed to be—my poem was—*there's no choice, any longer, I'm here to stay. In you I've found something; you lead the way.*"

"I don't care what it's supposed to be." Tears were dripping down my nose. Tears I didn't want him to see. Tears that had been waiting since that night at the party when my friends had walked away from me, since my mom had found out about the drinking, since volleyball and maybe even scholarships had slipped through my fingers.

With hands on my shoulders, he turned me to him and tried to wipe the tears slipping down my face. They wouldn't stop though, and his touch only caused me to choke on them harder.

"You said *I* inspired that poem."

"You did, I swear. You did." He gave up on my tears, his arms falling uselessly to his sides.

"Then how come she knows more than I do?" And then something else occurred to me: "Did she write it? Was that even you? Was it ever for us?"

"Yes! Of course it was for you! And I didn't give it to her, or read it to her or anything." His jaw tightened. "She just, she—"

"She what? She can read your mind?"

"No, she *takes* things. She thinks whatever I do she has rights to. You know, you've seen it."

I had seen it. She thought she had rights to him, too. All of him. That jealous girlfriend I swore I wouldn't be stood up inside my head and reminded me that Ivy had her own apartment, and whether Jay was there or not, they could do whatever they wanted. If our relationship was a well, this poem was special and buried deep. He'd let her get her hands on that, so who's to say what else he'd let her get her hands on? "What happened while I was grounded, Hawk?"

"Nothing happened, what are you talking about?"

I raised an eyebrow until it dawned on his face.

"You think." He pointed toward the door. "You think." Swallowing hard, his expression stiffened. "You think this is because we got together or something?" But now his tone wasn't so appeasing. "Eden, she looks through my stuff. She sings what she wants. I should've told her it was off limits, but I wasn't paying attention."

"You should've been! You let her take it and now it's not special anymore. Now *we're* not special anymore."

"This has nothing to do with us." He stressed each syllable. "I wrote every one of those words for you, why won't you listen to me? Hear what I'm saying, Eden, *please*. Have a little faith."

Maybe he didn't get me like I thought he had. Maybe he only saw girls like her, the girls who forced you to see them, the ones who took. I would never be that girl. I would never be the one who wanted an adrenaline rush, speeding across the parking lot or screaming on the stage. That's who he'd been drawn to his entire life, friend or not. He'd driven me to that parking lot, and expected me to get along with her, but I wasn't that girl.

He didn't see that, and he didn't see me.

Pushing him away, I said, "Leave me alone, Hawk. Just go."

"But, Eden." He gestured toward the door. "Your mom, it was going so well, her meeting Ivy—"

"I don't want her to meet Ivy." I said, swiping the water from my leaky eyes. "And I don't care how it's going. Everything was fine before you showed up."

That had slipped out and I wasn't sorry. I should have been, because it was mean and catty—also it was Billie's words in my head again—but it was also true. Maybe fine hadn't seemed good enough and maybe I'd wanted more, but this couldn't have been what I wanted. *This* felt miserable—all of it, everything. Javi was freaking out about State, which was my fault; I was grounded, which would never have happened if it weren't for him; and I'd let literally everyone in my old life down. I'd always been the good role model, but now I was the disappointment. Not to mention, my heart didn't feel very solid. It was shaky, and I was shaky, and that was his fault too.

"If it weren't for you, none of this would've happened," I repeated. There, how did that feel? I hoped a bit like hearing the poem your boyfriend wrote for you coming out of another girl's mouth.

He took a step back, and as my eyes dried with anger and determination, his went a little shiny in the light of *The Sonic Boom* sign above us.

"None of what?" he asked, tone now ripped apart, soft and torn.

"None of my life falling apart."

"What exactly are you saying?"

I ticked it off on my fingers. "If it weren't for you, there wouldn't have been a party, I wouldn't have gotten kicked off the volleyball team, I wouldn't have gotten grounded, my friends would be talking to me, and my brother wouldn't be giving me sad eyes every day."

He took a step back, stumbled almost, and all the emotion in me fizzled out. Because here I was, once again, the asshole. No better than Isaac and Billie and Wes. I shook my head to deny it, but it was true: *I'd had no problems before Hawk showed up.* I guess I was who I was, no matter what I looked like.

The door banged open, spitting my mom and Jerry out.

I opened my mouth to say something to Hawk, anything to maybe fix it—gah, that look on his face—but he wouldn't meet my eye.

"Eden?" my mom asked, looking back and forth between us.

"Take me home," I muttered, though I wasn't sure she heard me.

Hawk didn't move, and Jerry stayed by the door. My mom

stepped forward and reached for my hand. "It was a nice night, Hawk," she said. "Thank you."

He nodded.

Then he stood there, staring at the cement, while we left.

And then...

On Sunday, I did my homework with Reese.

On Monday, I sat at our empty lunch table, wondering where Billie, Wes, and Isaac were.

On Tuesday, I ate with Nat and Javi. They squeezed me onto an otherwise stuffed bench and left my head spinning with their food swapping.

Wednesday, I wrote and emailed Coach Warner a long-winded plea in the library, concurrently chewing off every one of my fingernails. Apparently, futzing with my watch was no longer enough to spin the anxious energy out of me.

Thursday, I drove to Isaac's to see if they were eating lunch there again, and his mom made me a tomato and basil grilled cheese. She asked about my mom and my brother, politely avoiding anything she'd heard about why I didn't know where my friends were.

Friday, I woke up dreading the weekend. Gaping long days

of hoping Hawk would call or text, when so far he hadn't, while also ignoring Ivy's strange non-apologies.

First: *It's not a big deal, just come over and help me with this origami penguin.*

The next day: *I need you to tell me this penguin looks good. It's going to be our first album cover.*

A few days later: *As much has happened between me and Hawk as between a tornado and a cyclone.*

I'd be mulling over what the hell that meant for days. Probably nothing, because this was Ivy we were talking about. Besides, odds were that if something was going to happen between them, it wouldn't have taken this long. I admit, I'd been in kind of a state when I'd accused him of that.

I dragged myself out of bed anyway, not bothering to look in the mirror and wonder about the magic. It didn't seem to matter anymore. I barely brushed my teeth, barely brushed my hair, barely chewed my peanut butter banana toast.

I barely felt awake on the way to school until I spotted Ivy at the steps. She stood at the base of them, in the center, the crowd morphing around her. She had to be waiting for me. I'd never in all my years seen her there and no other explanation made sense.

Before I could gauge whether I was still mad at her (for being who she was, I suppose), or what I might say, or if I just wanted to let the crowd pull me along past her, she stepped forward and pushed me through them, out onto the grass.

I caught myself on the bike rack and got a better look at her—hair a mess, tangled and unbrushed; pale eyes glassy. Way worse than I probably looked, mirror or no, magic or no.

It made me forget she'd shoved me, or at least made it less important.

"Are you okay?" I asked.

"You turned me in for nothing, you know. Hawk has literally never touched me. Never even looked at me that way. I could probably strip down in front of him and he wouldn't bat an eye. But do you care about the truth? No. You just get off on ruining lives."

"What are you talking about?" I wished there was a pause button, a rewind. "What would I even turn you in *for*?"

"Think foster care is something to write home about? Stupid bitch."

I blinked a few times as that sank in. Oh, *shit*. "But you're almost eighteen."

"They don't care how *almost* I am." She air-quoted the 'almost' and stepped into me. I stepped back. "They care that my mom's not around and I don't have a guardian." She stepped into me again. "And to think I almost felt bad for taking those lyrics. To think I even gave a shit it might've hurt your feelings, when you're just like everybody else." Then she spat on me, a wide spray that splattered across my face and shoulder.

I let it sit there for a moment, in shock, before wiping it off with my sleeve. "They can't just take you, can they?"

"All I did was borrow your song. Because it was good. Well, you know what? I hope you fucking rot." She wiped her eyes with both fists, smearing whatever leftover liner and mascara she'd layered on thickly the day before.

I took a tentative step toward her. "I didn't do it, I swear."

"Sure, just like Isaac didn't turn you in, huh?" With that, she was gone. I stared after her as she marched across the grass to Hawk's car, idling on the curb.

He couldn't believe I'd do that, could he? Would he ever speak to me again if he did? I might be mad, and confused, and sick of all this shit trouble I was knee deep in, but the thought of never speaking to him again…

Pulling out my phone, I swore to him via text that it hadn't been me, then stared at the screen, willing him to reply—who cared that he was driving her away from me, who cared that she was driving him away from me, who cared that I'd already driven him away from me.

"Eden?" Wes's voice carried over the stone railing. "You okay?"

I blinked to keep the tears at bay.

He pushed his way down the steps. "What happened?"

But when I could only flap my mouth and look back and forth between him and my phone, he moved so he could read the screen. I was confused. And numb. And horrified for her. What did foster care even mean for a seventeen-year-old?

Would she be moved to another city, away from Tony and Jay and Hawk and her band?

"What wasn't you?" he asked.

"Someone turned Ivy in, told the authorities she wasn't living at home." I looked up at him. "Isaac? Would he do that?"

"Isaac didn't even know that."

"But he was the one who turned me in."

"He didn't, though."

"Then who did?"

He shrugged. "We think it was Ivy."

"She wouldn't turn anyone in for anything."

"She's a strange girl, Eden. Who knows what she'd do."

I sighed, because I couldn't exactly argue with that even if I had the energy to.

"C'mon." He motioned his head toward the school. "Let's get to class."

26

The rest of Friday, my stomach chewed on itself with worry.

Worry over Ivy, the fact that Hawk hadn't responded to my text, and that I'd ruined my life twice over—the perfect vanilla life I used to have and the more brightly-colored one that started when I woke up looking perfect. Which had me wondering about the magic again. Only, there was no point in that, because if it was magic, it was like Jack's magic beans that ultimately brought him more trouble.

Friday night, I spent a lot of time in front of the mirror, trying to figure out why I ever thought I looked different. Also, stuffing my face with every high-calorie item I could find, because the only logical conclusion was that I hadn't woken up any different except high on myself, and look where that had gotten me.

Saturday morning, I decided to go back to the beginning, to the person I'd always depended on before.

Billie opened the door before my third knock, as if she'd known I was coming.

"Hey," she said.

"Want to sit?" I asked, motioning to the steps.

"You can come in," she offered, which meant her dad was having a good day. But I didn't need to disrupt it if this conversation went as poorly as our last. Living with MS didn't give him many to begin with.

"That's okay. It's nice out."

She raised an eyebrow because that was a bit of a stretch, but the bite in the air also kept me focused. Closing the door, Billie sat on the bottom step.

"Are you here for an apology?" she asked.

I looked at her sideways. "Not at all, actually."

"I keep thinking about it, apologizing. But then I think I shouldn't say I'm sorry if I'd do it again."

"I don't even care at this point. I just want things to be normal. With you guys *and* with Hawk and Ivy. I want it all and I don't understand why I can't have it all."

Her hands slipped down to her knees and she looked over at me. "Things would be normal if you didn't ditch us all the time. If you paid attention to what you were promising. Or if you even realized for one second what you'd missed. Like the swim meets."

She was right. I'd never thought about the swim meets. Friday nights. Billie by herself in the bleachers. "Fair. I'm sorry."

We were silent for a while, me flipping my watch around and Billie bent over playing with her shoelaces.

"Can I just ask you one question?" she finally asked.

"Sure."

"How did I end up on the bottom of your list?"

"How can you think you'd ever be on the bottom of my list?"

"How could I not?"

"But you're not even the type of person who thinks that way. You're impenetrable."

"Apparently not."

I studied her. "I'm here because you go to your best friend when you're at your lowest point. Even if you think your best friend is over you."

"I was never over you. It was just hard watching you piss away your perfect life, you know?"

My perfect life. I guess it probably seemed that way to most people. Stellar grades, good college prospects, bright future. Still, I'd wanted more. I'd wanted to feel that way on the inside, too. Ultimately, though, I couldn't get away from feeling like me. Nothing more, nothing less. Maybe there was no getting around that. Maybe feeling like yourself, even if that was messy and tangled and honest, was where a person found real perfection.

I let out a deep sigh and gazed at the oak across the street, still holding tight to a handful of its leaves. "You were never on the bottom of my list; I just got carried away. I felt like someone different and I let it carry me away."

"I'm sorry for every shitty thing I've done in this whole mess," she muttered.

And that's how two wrongs could make a right. When they faced each other and were honest.

I'd come to lean on her, because I guess it wasn't just that I hid behind her strength, but that it soothed me. So I did. I put my head on her shoulder, and she slipped her arm through mine.

27

Where *The Sonic Boom* was upbeat and lively, the playhouse was dressed in black and hushed with severity. Where *Sonic* didn't take itself too seriously, the playhouse commanded respect. Where *Sonic* allowed people to morph their tables and chairs however it worked for the crowd, the playhouse was lined with pews.

At least I was on the aisle, rather than stuffed between a jail of shoulders and knees. Wes was sitting a little too close on my left, Isaac next to him, and Billie on stage. She was speaking on the dangers of our mind prohibiting us from having healthy relationships. The others on the docket were a poet, a dancer, and two short one-woman shows.

Billie wasn't about acting or art, but about fact and science. It was kind of a wonder they loved her so much.

Her voice was melodic, though—euphonious, I thought with a pang—and she spun a more complicated web of thoughts originating from Mr. Keller's assignment, backed with studies she'd dug up and inspirational dares to take control of the relationships in our lives.

My focus rested on the noise more than the words. The noise and the visual, of course. I took a quick, stealthy picture that perfectly captured her up there—sitting on a stool, hands gesticulating with her punctuation, hair loose around her shoulders, the spotlight pulling all the loose strands to our attention and giving her a fuzzy, ethereal look.

Wrapping a hand around my not-so-dainty wrist, I figured nothing could make me ethereal, but there were worse things.

It would be worse to be so insecure that you were completely self-absorbed and utterly desperate.

It would be worse to be unaware and oblivious to your strengths because you were so focused on your weaknesses.

It could be worse. It *had* been worse.

Wes's eyes were glazing over, too, but then he'd seen her do this same performance a handful of times already. Constant. That's what he was. Steady.

Pulling out my phone, I texted him: *I'm sorry if I ever led you on.*

He was oblivious, his phone probably on silent, so I elbowed him and nodded to mine. Blinking at it, he took it from my hands and replied: *I'm sorry I was always such an idiot about it.*

I really love you a lot you know. You're my bff.

Well, your second bff.

I think mostly, I didn't want that to change. I was always kind of just living the role of Billie's sidekick, but with you I could be myself. Until you wanted me to be your girlfriend, then it was just another role I'd be playing, doing what was expected of me, you know?

I stared at the words before handing the phone to him, slightly stunned at how right they felt when I hadn't thought of them once before the moment they came from my fingers. Was that what started all this? My crisis of identity, and then the psych project...

Hands began to clap around us and we jumped to do the same. We'd planned to sneak out and meet Billie at the rear of the building, so I stuffed my phone in my pocket as the three of us slipped down the aisle.

"Listen," Wes whispered in my ear. "You wanted someone who would fight for you, who'd make a big fuss and come all the way, but so did I."

I handed him my phone, and Isaac stepped ahead to open the door that led to the lobby.

Wes read what I'd last written as Isaac led us across the frayed red carpet into the almost night. He unlocked his car with the key fob from twenty feet away, and Wes stopped me with a hand to my elbow.

"It means a lot that I was your safe place, where you could be yourself."

"Honestly, Wes, it says loads about you."

He flushed; I could tell even in the dim light. "More than I want you, I want someone who will fight for me too. If you're not going to be that girl, I'll keep looking for her. I'm okay with that."

I shoved into him. "Come on, let's go pick up our thespian

before she gets mobbed in the back alley."

"Yeah, right. I feel sorry for the person who'd try to mob her."

We were both sniggering as we slid into the back seat of Isaac's SUV. The car rolled quickly around the bent community theater, until the headlights caught Billie dead on.

"What'd you think?" she asked as she hopped in, twisting in her seat to look at me. Almost like she cared, almost like it mattered to her what anyone else thought. "Tell me you loved it?"

I laughed. "You don't need anyone to tell you they loved it. That's not why you do this, remember?"

She frowned, then slumped against her seat.

"Of course I loved it." I scooted up a little in my seat, feeling strange in this new place of needing to reassure her. "I got the coolest picture too."

Isaac caught my eye in the mirror. "There's one more performance, if you weren't listening."

Rolling my eyes away from him, I found the picture on my phone so I could send it to her.

"It's fine," Isaac said. "Wes and I were here for her when she needed someone, when you were too busy being there for yourself."

"Stop it," Billie said softly. "I want things to be normal again, and as long as you're lecturing her all the time, that's never going to happen."

"Actually," I corrected, "him lecturing me is exactly normal."

He winked at me as he parked at the café, where we were about to stuff our faces with pastries.

I hopped out on the asphalt. "Everyone's entitled to your opinion, right?"

Wes smirked and Isaac looked surprised, then considered it, then chose not to deny it. I was laughing pretty hard as we walked in, which made me feel like part of the world had righted itself.

Like I'd come home.

Monday

Monday after school, I knocked on Coach Warner's open door.

We never practiced on Mondays so I knew the girls weren't around. It was just a matter of catching him before he had to leave. Still, he ignored me while he finished what he was doing, as if he had all the time in the world.

Maybe he was more angry than I thought.

"Hi, Coach."

"Come in, Eden."

I sat down in his spare chair, my knees together and back straight, hands in my lap. "I know I'm not supposed to be at practice until the suspension is lifted, but I don't know how else to prove what it means to me, being a leader and co-captain of this team. Showing up to run balls for everyone—water, towels, whatever—it's the least I could do." I waited a beat, but he only folded his hands on his desk.

"Being there feels like the right thing to do. I know I won't be able to play Thursday, I'm not asking for an exception, it's just, as co-captain, I think it's important to be there for the team, in whatever capacity you'll let me."

"Have you spoken to your mom, like I suggested?"

"Sir, my mom is not the type to fight my battles for me. I mean, she knows I was suspended, if that's what you're worried about. I didn't lie to her or anything. But you're the only one who can change the rules. Did you get my email?"

"I did. I was waiting to hear back from your mom."

Huh?

Leaning forward, he said, "You know what, never mind. Be at the scrimmage tomorrow night. We lost so bad on Friday, there's no wiggle room left if we think we're going to make it to State."

"You mean... I can play?"

"Frankly, I can't take another minute of Javi and Nat without you. They've been in the worst moods." He stood with a smile, and I rose without one. I couldn't believe it was that easy. I just had to walk myself on in here?

"Thank you so much, Coach," I said, somehow without stuttering. "I really appreciate it. I can't tell you."

"You don't need to. Let's just finish this season with a bang."

"Of course, sir. I can't wait to get back out there."

He nodded, so I nodded, and then I was turning, resting a hand on the doorframe.

"Eden?"

"Yeah?" I looked back.

"I hate to say it, because I never thought I'd have to worry about you of all people, but know that if it happens again, if it's not your mom asking to help teach you a lesson, you will be out for the season."

My fingertips went numb.

Wait.

What?

If it's not my mom asking to help teach me a lesson?

Breathe, Eden. Focus. One thing at a time. Do not lose it. Do not ruin what you just won back. Clutching my hands into fists, I swallowed hard. "Of course, sir."

I heard him plop back down in his chair, and I forced my feet to move. To make it one step at a time, into the hall and out of eyesight. A little further, just around the corner. There, in the quiet of the emptied school hallway, I slid to the ground and stared at a scuffed gray tile.

That was supposed to feel good. To feel right. But now my stomach was sour. Sick.

My mom.

My own mother had turned me in.

29

I made sure my brother was in his room when my mom came home.

She'd brought Jerry with her and they filed into the kitchen where I was waiting. All my feelings over the last few weeks had built and culminated into a thumping in my ears, a rage in my chest, a horror that my own mother would throw me under the bus.

"What the fuck, Mom?" was how I greeted them.

"Eden!" She gave me one of her frowns, then asked Jerry if he'd like any tea.

"It was you who called Coach Warner, who turned me in."

Her frown leveled out and she looked at me steadily. Pursing her lips, she set the water boiling and pulled two cups out.

"I can't even look at you," I said. "I don't even know who you are anymore."

She rolled her eyes. "Don't be so dramatic."

She rolled her eyes. She thought my life, my team, my college applications, *State*, were eye-roll worthy? I let out a squeal. "Do you have any idea what kind of hell that put me through?"

My mom snapped her fingers. She actually snapped her fingers. Then said, "Don't blame me for your decisions. You

233

chose to be at that party, to drink, to risk college for goodness' sake! Of course I made sure to follow up! Consequences are important. No consequence means no change, and no change means more bad decisions. What else would you have expected from me?"

Jerry put a hand over hers, holding it flat against the counter.

"I would have expected you to have my back. I don't know. Talk to me about it. Ground me. I don't care, but it was one time and one beer and one mistake and you blew it out of proportion into this huge thing that it wasn't!"

"Natural consequences, Eden."

I felt like pulling my hair out. "One party, Mom. One time. No one gets punished for one mistake like you've punished me. Don't I get one free pass, after how perfect I've always been? It's not like I'm Ivy or something, who—" The words got caught in my throat.

She'd only do that to me, right? She wouldn't mess with anyone else's life. Surely not someone she barely knew.

But all those questions, their conversations over text. Now that I thought about it, my mom had totally been gathering information. Ammunition. Gauging the safety of her life.

I stood up straighter and took a step back. "You turned Ivy in too, didn't you?" Another step back. Then another, until I felt the wall. Bracing my hands against it, I tried to piece into place how this could have happened. How it could have gone so wrong. How I could have brought my mom and her righteousness to Ivy's door.

She leaned back against the counter and crossed her arms. "A young girl in high school throwing parties with adults is not appropriate."

"Screw appropriate!" I spit. "She was fine! She was managing! Jay is the closest thing to family she has!"

"Won't you feel better if the authorities agree?"

"No! I never felt bad about it! It was not your problem! *She* is not your problem! I'm your problem, just me!"

Then I felt it, the insistence in my core that something awful was happening. Like, really awful. Having nothing to do with it would be one thing, but it was a whole new terrible knowing I was partly responsible. A tugging, a sickness, a panic that I'd had a hand in something that might ruin someone else. Something that quite possibly couldn't be fixed.

If there was a way, I had to find it.

30

I borrowed my mom's car without asking.

Yeah, and I didn't feel bad about it.

I'd texted Hawk a few times, but he hadn't texted me back. Either he hated me for what Ivy thought I'd done, or he was waiting for a real apology for what I'd said. I owed him that, but every time I tried to form one, it hurt. Like I could hear those words coming out of her mouth again, flaunting how close she was to him, and how close I wasn't. That she was, and always would be, his number one.

It didn't matter now. I'd apologize up and down to find out what was happening. I'd show up at her door and get spit on, whatever, but decided the safest place to start would be the diner. If his mom was there, she might be able to tell me something, or at least give me an idea of what I was wading into. If nothing else, maybe she'd tell me where to find them.

Hugging myself against the wind, I hurried across the pockmarked blacktop and threw open the door to the diner. No one looked up. It was mostly empty, and quiet enough that I could hear the buzzing of the neon sign as I slid into the booth.

Hawk's mom pushed her way out of the kitchen with three plates on her arms and went the other way to drop them at a far table. Now that I knew Hawk better, I could see the resemblance, not in her face but in how she moved: smooth and measured, with purpose.

While I waited, I unlocked my phone and brought up my messages with Hawk, chewed on my lip, and tried to figure out what to say if she were no help.

I'm sorry. I take it all back. I'm a total ass and I meant none of it. This is all because of me. Including Ivy. It was my mom who called CPS. I'm SO SORRY I COULD LITERA

"Hi, sweets. How you holdin' up?"

The pain of that night still resonated so loud that I hadn't heard her coming. Flipping my phone face down on the table, I smiled up at her in greeting. "I'm okay. You?"

She grinned. "Happy as a clam. What can I get you?"

"Oh." I reached for a menu, but that was just pretense, which I was over, so I let my hand drop. "I don't know, anything, really. Fries and a Coke? But that's not why I'm here. I need to talk to Ivy or Hawk, but they're not returning my texts. It's really important." I wanted to ask if they hated me, but I winced instead. "I really messed up."

"We all do, at some point." Her voice was apologetic and soothing, as if I were a baby and this my first real life lesson.

"My mom turned her in. If it weren't for me…" I struggled to keep my emotion in check. My horror. The feel of a car spinning out of control, like back in that parking lot. "I have to try to fix it. I have to do something. Do you think if I showed up, if I found them, or waited at her apartment, that she'd talk to

237

me? Do you know anything? Would it help if I...if..."

If nothing, that was the problem. I could not conceive of any way to actually help the matter.

Hawk's mom tucked her pen and paper into her apron pocket and slid into the booth across from me. "For what it's worth, everything turned out okay. They got a hold of her mom and she had to fly in to sign some stuff, but it's all taken care of, for the most part. Crisis over."

I took a deep breath and the tension seeped out of me, slithering out my toes and across the linoleum floor. If that's all that happened, it was enough. If I couldn't get them back, at least she was okay. At least her life wasn't upended.

Spinning my phone on the old Formica, I studied the whirring pattern of my flowered case. "Do they hate me?"

"I'm sure not."

"I owe them both an apology."

"Hawk's pretty good with apologies."

"Ivy's not?"

"Ivy's predictable in her unpredictability." She stood back up. "Let me go grab you those fries and that Coke."

Leaning back in the booth, I deleted the text I'd started, and instead sent a simple *I'm sorry*. Then, to Ivy: *You were right. It was my mom. I'm miserable and sorry and it's my fault for being there. I'm sorry I was ever the type of girl you'd think would turn you in. I'm sorry if I've done anything to make you think I'd be such a shitty friend.*

As I waited for responses that might never come, I stared at the dark peach neon outside the window. Without realizing it, I'd picked the same booth Hawk and I had sat in the first time we'd been there. Framing the same shot I'd taken then, only this time without his face in it, I brought the neon into sharp focus.

I was done with blurry, with illusions. Clarity would be my goal from now on. Not what things looked like, but what they really were underneath, at their core.

Not what I looked like, either, but who I was beneath the noise.

31

Where you at? came the text back from Ivy.

At the diner, I replied, a bit of my earlier terror creeping back in. If they were together (likely) and both showed up (also likely), it would feel like an ambush. Certainly, they weren't going to walk in like nothing had happened, so would it be a confrontation?

No, if they wanted that, they'd already had plenty of chances.

Still, it wouldn't be like nothing happened.

I set my forehead on the table and tried not to poke my eyes out. Everything was going to be okay. Everything was *already* okay.

My phone pinged as Hawk's mom delivered my fries and Coke. With a squeeze to my shoulder, she was gone again, and I opened Hawk's response with trepidation.

Thank you. Much appreciated.

Okay. Well. That didn't give me much to go on, but it was something. More than I'd gotten yet. *How are you?* I asked, worried that if I didn't respond immediately, he'd slip through my fingers and disappear again into the void.

I'm all right.

I stared at his words, my fingers framing the screen and my

thumbs hanging over the letters, twitching with thoughts along the lines of *I miss you, I want you, come back to me.* But he was being distant.

You're still angry about what I said, I typed. *You should be. I wish I could take it all back.*

Why do you think I'm angry? he texted back.

Because you haven't been talking to me.

Because you told me I was ruining your life.

He stayed away to not ruin my life? *What are you then?* I asked. *If not angry?*

Sad. I'm sad you think I'd cheat on you. Sad that Ivy got to that poem (sorry for that, if I didn't say it that night. I was kind of in shock, too). Sad that I'm not good for your life.

I closed my eyes. What an awful thing to feel. *Never think that. It's me who hasn't been good for my life. Not you.*

It took a while, but by the time my fries were gone, I was staring at a reply: *I thought if I walked away you'd realize that wasn't true. Or at least, if it was, then your problems would be gone. Are your problems gone?*

Yes, I admitted. But shit, that sounded wrong. *But now I have this new problem where you're not around and I miss you. I miss us.*

I miss you too.

My turn again, but I didn't know where to take it. He was sad I thought he'd be the type to cheat on me, but here I sat, still believing she'd take the opening the minute he gave it to her. Did I think he'd give it to her?

I didn't *think* so, but we'd only been together and not together for a month. Though, he'd never done one thing to imply he would, so maybe it was time I start listening to his words and actions, instead of glazing over them for what I saw on the surface: the show she put on for me, where the two of them had all the history and went back a million years.

Before I could figure out how to condense all this into a text, Ivy plunked down across from me.

I swallowed, hard.

Last time I saw her, she'd spit on me. Here she was, though, breezing in, landing like she was glad to be here, like it had been a long day and she'd arrived to decompress.

"Okay, so truth is, I've been the shitty friend." She scraped a finger through the ketchup on my plate and stuck it in her mouth.

I raised an eyebrow.

"Well, first, everything's fine with CPS—that's Child Protective Services. They swooped in, scoured the place, interrogated us like you wouldn't believe—I'm surprised they didn't ask Jay for his tax returns and a piss test, but they didn't. Thank God. They couldn't get a hold of my mom, though, so it was touch and go for a minute. Had to get Marie here to save the day. She literally adopted me in the final hour, so now I'm legit. She said I can stay at Jay's, or she'll make me up a room at their place. Which I'm totally going to take her up on, just in case I want to hide from Tony or life or whatever. Two homes are better than one, right? But point is, don't worry about that. Water under the bridge, okay?"

I nodded. As I'd heard otherwise from Hawk's mom, I knew this wasn't exactly true, but maybe to Ivy they weren't exactly lies, but stories. What I wanted to get back to was why she was a shitty friend.

"Yeah, so. Hawk might not understand why you think something went down between us, but I do. I did that on purpose. He was mine, you know, forever. And even if he'd never date me, I wasn't totally kidding about that, about asking him from time to time, hinting. I always sort of thought of him as my backup plan. Or like someday he'd come around and ultimately we'd end up together when we were like forty and ready to settle down. Honestly, who's to say you're even a threat to that? So it was dumb anxiety on my part, but I was jealous. He's never spent so much time with another girl, or talked about another girl, and then that poem. I mean, honestly, swoon, amiright? You cannot blame me for grabbing that up as soon as I came across it. But you should know, if there's any doubt, that he didn't know I took it until you did. His stuff has always been my stuff and my stuff has always been his stuff and you changed that too, in like two weeks, which is ridiculous, let me say, but whatever."

Another swipe through my ketchup, then she pulled the plate toward her.

"I did it all on purpose, so you would question your place. And that was super shitty and I probably got what I deserved, because when you were gone, he was miserable, and that was a serious buzzkill. But also, I was miserable, and I wasn't expecting that. I've literally never known what it was like to have a girlfriend, and I guess I really liked it."

Finger pad to some loose salt and debris on my plate, into the ketchup, to her mouth.

"So, what do you say?"

I blinked.

"Truce? Start over? Friends? I'll do my damndest to keep my hands off your boyfriend."

I liked having her too, even with her lies and stories. Billie and my mom would tell me not to be friends with someone like that, but if I went in with eyes wide open, well, if Hawk could do it and not be fooled, couldn't I? Honestly, maybe it would be good for me, force me to stay the course and see her for what she was—vulnerable and trying—rather than the illusion she put out in the world.

Ultimately, here was one more opportunity to right something, if only I'd say so, which is what I wanted—my old life and new, together.

I sighed. "If he'll even still have me."

She rolled her eyes. "He's *crazy* about you. It's disgusting. You should hear the latest poem he's been working on—don't tell him I read it, he made me promise not to snoop anymore, but give me a break, he should know better." She leaned forward with a laugh. "He'll have to literally put a lock on it to keep me out. You're his muse, he's mine, that's just the way it is. How am I supposed to write music without his words?" She waved a hand in the air and went on.

She went on and on and on, and we laughed and talked boys, and she reassured me again and again, until it almost felt like Hawk and I were already back together. So at least there was that.

One more relationship right.

32

I drove home thinking of Ivy's newest outfit, hair, and makeup plans for her next show. Or her new series of shows, as she was calling it. My song—she'd actually named it *Eden's Song*, so now everyone knew, which was embarrassing and almost worse—was to be the highlight of the series. Everyone loved it, she'd said, so much that Jay was working on getting some studio space to record it and they might do a YouTube video. She wanted a whole new look for the video, and she wanted it to feel like love and yearning and hope and new relationships, because was there anything better than that?

My head was spinning as I made my way inside the house, because that's the effect Ivy had. The kind of spinning that made you smile, even when you walked in to see your traitorous mom waiting up for you on the couch.

I suppose the fact that she hadn't hunted me down when I took her car should get her some points. If I were in the mood to offer up any.

"You left before dinner," she said. There was a plate of corned beef hash and hash browns on the coffee table in front of her. My favorite meal, albeit slightly repetitive.

The ingredients weren't staples in our kitchen, which meant she'd walked to the store for them, as I had the car. Or maybe Jerry drove her. Either way, a serious peace offering.

I eyeballed it, wishing it didn't sing such a euphonious tune.

"Reese is in your bed," she whispered. "I couldn't talk him out of it."

I slipped her car keys into the bowl next to the TV. "What's that about?"

"He heard you yelling and is worried about you, and me, and the state of the world." She patted the seat beside her. "Can we talk?"

"I don't know, did you ask if we could talk before making decisions involving my friends? Friends I knew more about than you did?"

She sighed. "Fair enough. However, there were numerous safety issues there."

"She's seventeen, Mom. Not twelve."

"When you're my age, Eden, seventeen no longer seems so worldly."

I crossed my arms but didn't leave the front entry tile. "You can talk to me from here."

"Your brother is less sure of you, and now he's less sure of me, and that makes him less sure of everything." She put a hand up. "I'm not blaming you for that; I'm just letting you know what's going on. I think a little reassurance from you, that you and I will be speaking to each other again someday, would go a long way."

"You might not blame me, but you've always put it on me to

be perfect for him. I'm sorry I slipped up here, but life isn't perfect, and someday he's going to have his own reckoning if you try to shield him from the truth, just like I did."

"I've never tried to keep you from the truth, Eden. What a thing to say. I protect you, what do you expect? I'm your mother."

"I expect you to have my back. If someone else had turned me in, fine, natural consequences, but I should know that when I come home, I'm safe, that I can trust you. What if Jerry hadn't been there? What if I'd come home and told you all about it, would you have turned me in then? I mean, honestly, we all make mistakes at some point, don't you want me to feel like I can confide in you?"

"Yes, of course. It kills me if I've ruined that, but the Ivy situation was as much about concern for her safety as it was for yours. Also due to some things she said when we were texting. As a mother, I couldn't hear all that and not make sure she was safe."

"You could have at least told me, so I didn't blame everyone else." I moved to the floor in front of the coffee table, and reached for the fork and napkin. She shoved the plate across the wood, closer to me.

"I wouldn't do it differently, and I'm sorry about that, but I will tell you next time, okay? I'll give you a heads up and maybe, if you can think of some other solution, I'll consider it. But regardless, I'll tell you so you know."

"You really believe that was the right thing?" Forking a bite of corned beef hash—I mean, you can't let it get cold—I realized how hungry I was.

"I really do. And it's not like I didn't agonize over it. But there are people whose job it is to assess these situations and—"

I held up a hand. "Okay, I get it."

"I texted Ivy and apologized. So hopefully it won't be a problem between you two. That was never my intention."

"What about Isaac?" I mumbled through the hash browns. "Between the volleyball thing and this, I called him a weasel no less than a million times."

She raised an eyebrow. "I suppose I could."

"Nah. He's kind of a weasel anyway. I'll take care of it."

"I love you, you know. I worry. A lot. It's what moms do."

"I know. I love you, too." I swallowed too big a bite and coughed.

"Let me get you some water."

"How about a door?" I called, as softly as I could but so she could still hear me in the kitchen.

"Don't push it," she said when she came back. "You smuggled a boy into your room to roll around on your bed when you were grounded, and now have the easiest access out your window until it gets repaired."

"We were not—"

This time she put up a hand. "I don't want you to try and

justify exactly what line you did or did not cross in an obviously heated make-out session. I just want the door off your room a bit longer."

Fine. I would gulp down my water and finish my hash and accept her peace offering the same easy way that Ivy had accepted mine. I would put that kind of karma out in the world and hope that the rest of my life reaped its return. I would be soft and forgiving now, instead of black and white.

Besides, there were plenty of other places to have rolling-on-the-bed, steamy make-out sessions with Hawk, if he'd still have me. Ivy had two bedrooms now, according to her, and she'd definitely let me use them. I smiled. I wouldn't use her bedrooms, and there was no second one anyway, but it still made me smile.

"What?" my mom asked.

"Nothing. I'm just...happy, I guess."

"Good. That's what I like to hear."

"Well, don't think all your tattling had anything to do with it."

"No?"

"No." And I wasn't going to think about that too long, because if I did, and it had, well, just no.

She offered to take my dishes, and we stood at the same time. She kissed my forehead, said good night, and I stumbled down the hall, falling into bed next to my brother. Emotions were the worst. They could really tire a girl out.

Resting my head against Reese's, I inhaled that little brother smell. It wasn't so good, but it wasn't so bad either. He shifted and turned, so I backed up a bit to see him better.

"Is Mom bad now, too?" he whispered, in his sleepiest voice.

"No one is bad, Reese, remember what I said?"

"But I've never seen you so mad, Edie."

"Go to sleep and we'll talk about it in the morning."

"But we won't. No one ever tells me anything."

This quieted me for a moment. I'd spent my life protecting him just like my mom protected me, but he was old enough now that the truth was better. Facing reality was better than skating along on top of it. He needed honesty and nuance instead of all this good and bad, because that's what life was: nuance.

"I will this time, I promise. I'll tell you everything, how it is, from now on."

That seemed to settle him, as his eyelids drifted back closed. "Is it morning now? Why do you smell like breakfast?"

Tuesday

Lunch, the next day.

I sat next to Wes, shoving into him so he would scoot down, until I was directly across from Isaac.

"So." I pointed a carrot at him.

"So."

"I need to apologize."

"In that case, I'm all ears."

"I'm sorry that I thought your need for truth and righteousness would overcome your loyalty. I now know you weren't the one who turned me in to Coach Warner."

"You *now* know," he repeated. "As in, you didn't come to the realization I'm a good guy on your own, but rather, in the face of solid evidence, you forgave me?"

"Unfortunately, yes."

"Okay, I'll take it." And he went back to his coagulated cafeteria pizza.

I stood and rounded the table, motioning for him to get up. "I am really, truly sorry for having so little faith in you," I mumbled into our hug. "I guess, honestly, it was myself I didn't have much faith in, and feeling like everyone else had lost faith in me too." I cleared my throat, pulled away, and sat back down.

"No one lost faith in you." He dug into his pocket and handed me a piece of paper. "As usual, Billie is done with her semester project months early. I think maybe you should read it, since you weren't paying attention Saturday."

I made a face at him and unfolded the neat square. Billie busied herself with eating.

Wilhelmina Wright
Psychology of Perception
Relational Dependency

I have long believed men and women depend on each other too much, that they find their identity within the scope of romantic involvement to a point in which it hurts them as individuals. To be strong and independent, to move toward who you are, to your highest achievement, you must not allow yourself to be held back by anyone else's tethers.

As you can see from my list, I saw the wrong side of what a relationship brought to the table. And due to some things that went on in my life throughout the course of this project, along with my list which I originally thought to be on the pros and cons of the guy most girls would call my boyfriend, I realized I had been, in actuality, tethered to someone the whole time.

Refusing to believe a guy could help me or support me or get me where I wanted to go, I overlooked the fact that my best friend was doing all those things. The pros on my list easily described us, until recently. I had been tethered all along, but to a friend, because I'd trusted such a relationship would not derail me like a romantic one might.

Only, it did. And as my relationship with her derailed, as I recognized the effect it had on me being more in the category of my cons, I realized it wasn't about boy/girl or tether versus freedom. It was about the inside of a person, about respect and mutual admiration.

Relational dependency is healthy insomuch as it reflects the intentions of the two people involved. If I am always looking out for you, and you are always looking out for me (not you and me exactly, Mr. Keller, you know what I mean), then there are no tethers, but something better even than freedom. Really, there's a balance of support, and that's what I should have been focused on this whole time.

You asked how this project changed us, and for me it's that I can welcome a hand now, knowing it isn't trying to pull me back. Rather, the right hand, the one whose intentions only I can discern, will boost me forward.

There was a little note at the bottom that she'd scribbled to Isaac: *You have always been that right hand, and I never realized it. Thank you for being you, and thank you for letting me be me.*

"Aw, I'm so happy for you guys." But I had tears in my eyes.

Billie met them with her own. "Don't think I'm saying you were the wrong hand, Eden. I just didn't realize I had more than one right hand for me, until yours wasn't there anymore."

"I'm sorry it got to that point, where mine wasn't there."

She slid her arm through Isaac's. "I'm not."

I folded up her paper and gave it back to him. "You carry that around with you wherever you go?"

He cleared his throat, then asked, "Have you talked to Hawk?"

I looked down at my chili, the squares of cheddar on top loosening into blobs. "Not exactly. Not yet."

"Don't string him along too long."

"I'm not meaning to string him along."

"Then fight for him, Eden." Wes nudged me. "Honestly, fight for something, huh?"

With a heavy sigh and an eye roll for good measure—not that his prodding was really making me do it—I pulled out my phone and texted Hawk: *Meet me outside the locker rooms tonight? I have something for you.*

~

The scrimmage was exhilarating. I hadn't realized how much I'd missed being physical, throwing my body around on the court, doing what it was meant to do.

And I owned it. I was back. No more thinking dainty and petite, but strong and solid and *effective*.

It was how I'd been formed and I might as well embrace it.

Javi and Nat tackled me after—the three of us had been unstoppable: bumper, setter, spiker.

"Thank God," Javi breathed.

"We thought for a second we'd lost you forever," Nat seconded.

"We thought we'd lost State forever!"

I guess after so many years, all the cogs in the machine were well-oiled the way they were. Take one out and it ground to a halt.

Take any one of us out and it would've ground to a halt.

"Eden," Nat tugged at my braid. "You won't believe what we're doing this weekend."

"What?"

"Hookah lounge!" Javi said, while raising the roof.

I raised an eyebrow at her. "Dork."

She dissolved into laughter. "Dorks don't go to hookah lounges."

"But you do."

She stuck a tongue out at me. "I checked out their menu online. They have chai latte flavor."

"You better keep your lung capacity up for State, ladies."

Nat formed an "O" with her mouth. "Good point. I might have to refrain now."

"Noooo!" Javi whined.

"You just want to go because you want to land my brother, so who cares about the hookah, really?"

"Your brother's in town?" I asked. Which made sense. He'd always been a smoker. Of just about everything.

Javi flung her backpack over her shoulder haughtily. "I do not, of course I do, want to land your brother. What?"

I sat down on the bench with a snicker.

"We gotta run," Nat said, shoving Javi forward. "So help me."

"I do not, of course I do, have a chance now that I have boobs."

"He's not a boob man."

"He is. You can think he's asexual all you want, but I guarantee he's a boob man."

"Gross! Stop talking about my brother and boobs. Unless you're talking about his boobs."

"He doesn't have boobs. He's tight."

"I SAID GROSS."

This continued on until their voices faded, and my smile faded with them. There were a handful of other stragglers, but by the time I got out of the shower, the room was silent. And as I walked by the mirrors back to the lockers, my reflection caught me for a moment.

Maybe I did look the same as I always had, but now I was kind of okay with that. Everyone had imperfections, so why should I be ashamed of mine? I was the only one who seemed to care a lick about them in the first place.

The truth was, my strengths were mine too, and I'd worked with them a long time, which meant I also knew how to best use them. If I worked so hard to highlight my strengths for others to see, why wasn't I also highlighting them for myself?

I pulled my grandpa's not-so-magic watch back over my wrist and promised him I'd get it fixed soon. Combine my temporary belief in magic with an out-of-the-box psych project and a desperation to be perfect, and I'd turned my life upside down. Which was maybe what it needed.

With another smile, I threw my bag over my shoulder, and swung out into the hall, teeth on my lip in worry that Hawk wouldn't be there. That he would've decided not to come.

But he was leaning against the wall, legs crossed and one hand in his pocket. The other held his phone and when the door shut behind me, he looked up.

Putting a hand to my towel-dried hair, I resisted the urge to say, *I know I look terrible; I forgot a blow dryer.* Instead, I grinned. "I brought you something."

He pocketed the phone and pushed himself off the wall.

"First, let me say, one final time, how mortified I am that I blamed all my problems on you. That was really"—I looked straight into his eyes—"*really* not cool of me. I'd do anything to take it back."

He cleared his throat. "It's okay. These last few weeks, watching you with Wes at lunch and in the halls, when I realized all the connections you had to him, I finally got it. How you must have felt when she sang that song."

"How about we forget it ever happened." I took a step

toward him. "And try not to let it happen again."

"I told Ivy she wasn't allowed to take anything I didn't hand over to her personally."

Yeah, about that... "How about we just trust each other? How about next time I just believe you when you say it was unintentional and you love me the most?"

He grinned. "I do, you know. The most."

I grinned back. That was perfect. He did have a way with words. We stepped closer to each other and he put a hand on my waist. Dropping my bag and purse on the floor, I slid my arms under his and tilted my head back for his lips to land where they were meant to be.

They'd never fit more perfectly, and I wanted to hold that feeling of his bottom lip between mine. But he pulled it out and came back again, soft and slow and aching, until the last weeks of being apart caught up to us.

"So," he whispered, "what did you bring me?"

I pictured the Speedo and bikini I had stuffed in my purse. They fit quite nicely in there, along with my confidence.

Note to self: Never leave home without it.

Also by J Mercer:
Triplicity
Reviews & Excerpt

"*Triplicity* is an engrossing chronicle that is recommended for mystery and thriller enthusiasts as well as those who enjoy strong, proactive, often rebellious teen protagonists more than capable of taking matters into their own hands. It should also be noted that although the main characters are teens, *Triplicity* should not be limited to young adult audiences. The depth of characterization, flavors of romance, adult confidences, and alternating viewpoints keep this story lively and involving for all ages."

— *D. Donovan, Senior Reviewer, Midwest Book Review*

"The authentic characters, snappy writing style, and compelling plots make it an ideal selection for any high-schooler."

— *Manhattan Book Review, 5 star review*

"A great balance of mystery and intrigue with a truly fabulous cast of characters."

— *San Francisco Book Review, 5 star review*

Day 1: Boarding

Boat departs at 4:00 p.m.

Navy

Masses of people stood in line to board the incubator in front of me. Sorry, cruise ship. But honestly, the thought of so many bodily fluids in such a confined space made my stomach churn.

Double-checking that my hand sanitizer was still in place, I bumped my backpack higher on my shoulder and stepped away from my mom's fiancé, who was chatting up a blue-haired old lady. Facing my mom, I decided it was as good a time as any to start up our fight again. She couldn't get away from me here.

"If we keep moving like this," I started, "I'll never be kissed." There'd been one guy in Houston I'd had hopes for, but after this vacation we were headed to Kansas City. I might only be sixteen and five-sixths, but at this point it felt like I'd be voting first.

"You do the kissing then, Navy." My mom caught the eye of an officer at the next checkpoint and smiled, smoothing her hands down the front of her black jumpsuit. She was always worried about her first impression and always deferential to those in uniform.

I reached behind her and tightened her halter top, thankful at least she hadn't picked the leopard print. It was a good thing we were getting out of Texas before its fashion sense could get too many claws in her.

My mom's normal go-to attire—conservative diamond studs, fitted sweaters with pencil skirts, and sleek suits—would curl a lip at sharing suitcase space with a glorified onesie in leopard print.

Her attention hopped from the officer to Guy, my soon-to-be stepdad. "Solve your own problems, dear. Before they can solve you."

"No, Mom. Just, no." She would never get it; everyone wanted to kiss her. Somehow, she pulled off rich and cultured while still approachable, where my resting face was icy at best.

A girl couldn't help her resting face, and it took a long time for people to get past that. Plus, I was too picky, or so my mother said. I wanted real emotion, not just chemistry, and I definitely didn't want to get it over with, which is what she kept telling me to do.

"Anyway, this move,"—always moving, I should add—"it's about stability too."

Guy let out a huge laugh, and the old lady's hat bobbled in the air as her shoulders shook. My mom and I shuffled forward, neither of us bothering to notify him he was holding up the line. It didn't matter; this was the Godzilla of lines. Take any ride at Disney on the busiest day of the year, and it wouldn't top this one: through a vast building (stand here, punch that, sign this, rude hands gesturing you impatiently over there like you'd done this before and had any idea what they wanted with you), out into a human holding tank, up and back and up and forth inside a humongous steel cage, until finally we reached the deck that wrapped around the massive boat.

We were cattle. And we were being herded into an incubator.

Shaking my head of it, I begged her, "Please, please, *please* don't make me switch high schools again. This is the last one, okay? Can you manage two years in Kansas City?"

"If you insist, love." My mom patted the back of my head, then dropped her hand to my shoulder and kneaded it. With her attention focused elsewhere, it was her usual absent-minded pep talk. "If you don't want to see more of the world."

Shaking her off, I took a few steps forward. Guy was still flirting with the old lady and people were starting to grumble behind them, so I went back for his stuff and tapped him on the shoulder. His black turtleneck made him look even more pompous than he was, but this lady was eating it up same as my mom had. When I was back at her side, I whispered, "If you get sick of Guy, we stay in Kansas City anyway. Got it?"

She extended her diamond-studded right hand to shake mine. "Got it."

Wrapping my bare fingers around her chilled palm and the collection of old rings resting along her knuckles, I wondered if she actually loved this one.

Isaiah

The ship was so big. As big as a mountain. But I was used to twenty people on a mountain, not a million people inside one.

I craned my neck to get a better look at the girl ten or so people ahead of us. Of course, Gram thought I was watching the pretty boy with the sparkling teeth and preppy outfit.

"Keep your eyes in your head, Zay," she muttered.

It didn't matter how many times I told her I liked girls. She couldn't imagine why else I'd want to work with an all-male ranch staff in the middle of nowhere, Montana.

The girl's blonde hair was a shiny mane, and her outfit—dark skinny jeans, a white tee, and huge turquoise earrings—was perfect: no frills, no bullshit.

Gram swatted me with her purse. I glared at her.

"Nice to have a week off, Zay?" My great-aunt Ethel asked.

We were here on her dime, bought company for an old woman, so I muttered out a response and went back to the hair. My fingers twitched to feel it. Not in a creepy way, but brushing out horses was the most relaxing part of my day.

"He's got more 'an a week," Gram said. "I'm not sendin' him back."

My throat dried up. She couldn't be serious.

"I mean it too." Nodding, she grabbed her suitcase. Marched forward a few paces.

I hurried after her. "I can't quit in the middle of a summer with no notice. Ike needs me."

"I gave Ike your notice the day you left. He knows."

"Why would you do that?"

Hands on her hips. "You had a girlfriend yet?"

"Yes!"

"Yeah, right. I know how many of them're up at that ranch."

"Gram, I'm watching that blonde girl, okay?" I pointed over her head. The boy who was way too preppy for me turned. He put up a few fingers and waved.

"That prissy one with the frown?" Ethel asked. "She looks mean."

"Oh, he's just tellin' me what he knows I wanna hear. Tellin' time's over, Zay. You need to get your life together."

"What's wrong with my life?" What I had was what I wanted. All I'd ever want. My fist clenched. I couldn't lose the ranch, not after I'd lost everything else.

"Them boys aren't gonna make you a family, and that ranch ain't gonna make you a future." She shuffled her feet forward.

I pulled my cowboy hat down. The blonde was slipping inside the ship anyway. "They *are* my family, and if being a grunt ranch hand is my future, I'm happy with that."

"I'm your family," she snapped. "And you're happy with it because you're seventeen and you don't know no better."

"Gram, please?" It was a desperate whisper.

"It's all the poor boy has left," Aunt Ethel pointed out, not looking at me. Not even for a second. As if I might miss that I was the poor boy she was talking about.

Gram crossed her arms. "Building his future is more important than what he does or does not have left."

"Other people we know have been gay," Aunt Ethel said. "Jeannie from the corner, for example, and you never worried about her future."

Gram glared at her. "Jeannie wasn't my grandson."

"Then make me a deal," I said, because this was something we did.

"Yes." Aunt Ethel smiled before turning back to Gram. "He gets a girlfriend, you let him go back."

Gram looked like she was face-to-face with a skunk. "What's a girlfriend gonna prove?"

"For one, it'll prove he likes girls."

"He can right fake that. Anyway, there's more 'an one reason I don't want him at that ranch."

"Give the boy some hope, Liza. He's only seventeen. He's still got time to work his life out."

Gram eyed me for a full two minutes. I counted the ticks in my head while studying the wooden decking, how it barely moved beneath my feet. Hope was suddenly the color of that girl's hair, and I talked myself into wanting the rest of her too, no matter what she ended up being. Because now, with Gram's curt nod, it seemed she was the only way I'd get back home.

Jesse

"I am not sleeping there," I said, throwing my suitcase on the one queen bed in the room and heading to the patio doors that led to a tiny deck. "Mom should be sleeping there, and I won't take her spot."

We were pulling away from port, and the skyline of Seattle stretched in front of me like a postcard or a puzzle. Futzing with the lock, I opened the door and stepped out to take a picture.

"Only for photos!" my dad called, a reminder not to use my phone. I could barely hear him, though, over the hum of the engine and the slapping of the waves against the boat. The downside to taking a ship to sea? No cell towers, roaming charges, and very expensive Wi-Fi.

I went back inside but left the door open for the fresh air. Well, arguably fresh. The odor of big city tainted the briny scent coming off the water, but soon enough we'd be able to fill our noses with it.

"Stupid to have them pull out that couch for you every night." Unzipping his luggage, my dad motioned me over and nudged my suitcase. "I won't spoon you, don't worry."

Sliding into the little hall by the bathroom, he returned with hangers. As he slid his dress clothes onto them, I could tell by the muscles hardening his brightly-colored biceps that he wasn't as cool with the whole situation as he looked. Why was I giving him a hard time anyway? She was leaving us both.

I swallowed. "Why'd she surprise us with a trip if she wasn't going to come?"

"So she wouldn't have to face us."

My crisp dress shirt crumpled in my fist.

"If we were there when she was moving out, we'd have made her feel more guilty." His words were radio static, strange and wrong and scraping. I regretted asking the question.

He motioned for the items I'd hung up, then went back to the closet. A few moments passed, longer than it took to hang a few shirts on a rod. I'd never seen my dad cry, but there'd been a few times on the drive here when I thought he might lose it. The thing was, though, her stuff had been in all the right places when I'd been packing, and she'd been there when we pulled out of the driveway. For all we knew, no matter what she said, she might still be there when we got back.

A knock shook the door, and with three strides, Dad had it open. A short, slight man stood in front of him, in yet another uniform. There'd been no shortage of people today and no shortage of uniforms.

"Hi sirs. I will like to introduce myself to you, your cabin attendant this week." He nodded, but I knew my dad couldn't hear him over the accent. Which made them even, as likely our cabin attendant couldn't hear my dad over his tattoos. Most people couldn't.

I stepped up to shake his hand and repeated him for my father's sake. "You're our cabin attendant this week?"

He pumped my arm and nodded with the same beat.

"Anything you need. I help. Every night I pull down sheets. Turn down service, chocolates. I bring your bags to your door. I take them out for you at end of week. Have a question? You find me." He motioned up and down the hall, like that's where he'd be.

Checking his nametag, I said, "It's nice to meet you, Danilo."

"Da-NEE-lo," he corrected my pronunciation with a smile.

"I'm Jesse Kowalski." I thumbed toward my dad, who'd slipped back into the tiny hall. "That's my dad. People call him Wally."

Dad rolled his eyes and turned away. He hated when I chatted with people.

"Is only the two of you?" he asked, peering in as if he could see into our past two weeks.

Dad made a garbled noise, and I nodded.

"I will split bed, okay?" He motioned toward it.

"Oh. You can do that?"

"Yes, sir. Sorry to have made mistake."

"There was, um, no mistake," I assured.

"I'll split when you are at dinner, yes?"

"That's great, Danilo, thanks." Nodding, I hung a hand on top of the open door. "Hey, where you from?"

"Philippines, Jesse. You?"

"Omaha, Nebraska. Ever heard of it?"

"No, sir."

"Center of the U.S. Land-locked. Know what I mean?"

He shook his head, a wrinkle creasing between his brows.

"So far inland, no sea in sight." He seemed a little confused, so I moved on. "You leave anyone behind in the Philippines?"

"I don't think those are the kinds of questions he was talking about, Jess," my dad grumbled from the bed.

"I have wife. Five boys. One girl. Many sisters too."

"How long are you here then, working on the boat?" Dropping my arm, I leaned against the door. "When do you go home?"

"Six months. Then home six months."

"Yeah? The pay good?"

"Oh, yes. Lots of money for easy living in the Philippines."

I nodded. That's what I'd do. I'd pretend my mom was working on a cruise ship. Six months on and six months off sounded like a way better reason for her not to be here. Maybe then it wouldn't hurt so bad, the tears my dad hadn't shed that were scraping me raw anyway.

Navy

"Don't be a party pooper, Navy. The teen lounge has all sorts of fun activities planned for your enjoyment."

"That's exactly the problem, Mom. The people who say they've planned fun activities for my enjoyment don't know what fun is."

We were waiting in line (ugh, the lines!) to enter the dining room, where apparently we'd eat every meal at the same table with the same people, probably a bunch of old ladies, and I'd have to listen to Guy chatting them up seven nights in a row.

At least he'd known how to find the dining hall. As he kept saying, this wasn't his first rodeo. Mom and I had been walking in circles before he'd caught up to us. Granted, we'd been distracted with the fancy staircases and glitzy central piazza, but the Venetian Ballroom was also situated in a rather shadowy alcove.

And Venetian it was, if I took the paintings hung along the paneled wooden walls to be accurate: boats and water, squat buildings and looming mountains, a woman in a poufy blouse and full skirt bent in an awkward position over a copper bucket.

I followed my mom, who followed Guy, who followed a host to our table. The host pulled out a chair for my mom, and the waiter, already in position, pulled one out for me.

"Thank you." I nodded. He was tall and broad with intense, beady eyes.

"You're welcome, Miss." Oh, but he had a lovely accent.

The many different native tongues were an unexpected bonus of this cruise. Like Vegas, where each nametag listed a home state, the nametags on this ship listed a home country. How many languages could I keep track of at one time? And how much could I soak up in a week?

"Guy!" an old lady shrieked from behind me, before I could awkwardly ask our host how they'd say 'You're welcome' in

Hungarian. "What a surprise!"

"Ethel! So lovely to see you again!" Guy stood up and took both of her red-tipped hands in his. "We couldn't have planned it better!"

He pulled out her chair, and I looked up to find she wasn't as old as her voice made her sound, maybe sixties. Ten years older than Guy and twenty more than my mom. She was a hippy kind of trendy with long, curly gray hair. There was a cute old lady with her, and a teenager. A male teenager, in fact, with lips. That covered two of the three necessary kissing ingredients, the third being some sort of emotional connection. Could I find that in a week?

He tipped his cowboy hat at me. It was a nice one too, if I'd learned anything in the five months we'd been in Texas.

"Who's with you, Guy? I think we saw this lovely girl in line." Ethel squinted at me. "Zay, didn't we see her in line?"

The cowboy with the wholesome farm boy face reached his hand over the table. "Isaiah. They call me Zay."

I didn't take it. Who knew if he had ever-a-virus, or whatever it was going around. "Navy Carmichael," I replied instead, forcing out a smile so I wouldn't seem completely rude.

Isaiah's hand hung there while Guy and Ethel finished introductions. The old lady was Isaiah's grandmother Liza, and Ethel was her sister. Then there were the vomit-worthy congrats-I-didn't-even-know-you-were-engaged coos.

"How do you know each other?" I asked Guy and Ethel. "I mean, how *would* you have known he was engaged?"

Ethel and Liza stared at me, and my mom patted my thigh. "Baby, it's just something people say to be nice."

"We met on my first cruise, many years ago." Ethel smiled at Guy. "He showed me the ropes, and we've been bumping into each other ever since. That was Turkey and Greece, right?"

Dang, how come we had to be going to Alaska?

"It was. You won the jackpot that trip." He elbowed her. "Ethel's a Bingo shark, ladies. Watch out for her."

My mom leaned closer to Guy but set her interested face on Ethel. "You'll have to show me some tricks. I've heard Bingo is exhilarating."

"You've never played?" Liza asked.

"Don't worry," Mom assured her. "I plan to start this week. I hear that's where the action is on these cruise ships."

Ethel and Liza studied her with blank faces. I agreed. She didn't seem much for action, with the perfectly smoothed hair and pearly fingernails. A slim white jacket was buttoned over her black jumpsuit, and a dainty gold necklace hung from her neck. The whole vibe screamed proper, high-class lady.

You could hardly see the pastor's wife anymore, or the Southern belle straight off a good old-fashioned plantation. Honestly, I missed them both.

Jesse

There were two chairs left at our assigned dinner table, and they sat between a cowboy and the most intimidating girl I'd ever seen. *Hi, I'm Navy*, she'd said, *Navy Carmichael*. She had a spattering of yellow-gold freckles on her face, the same color as her hair, which was rich and shiny like liquid gold, and they accented a severe expression I couldn't shake.

She had perfect posture, refused my handshake, and looked like she belonged with the fancy white tablecloths, fresh flower centerpieces, and glass goblets for water, of all things. Fifteen pieces of silverware per plate, each of us with a coffee cup, and a basket of rolls in the center of the table covered with more white cloth.

Back home, my mom threw a stack of buttered bread on a plate and called it a day.

As everyone introduced themselves, I tugged my t-shirt sleeve down over my tattooed bicep and slid my palm over the mustache on the back of my elbow. Rites of passage, seeing as the family business was an ink shop.

Navy caught me, and I played it off by strumming my fingers a bit. I couldn't read her expression, but no doubt she was labeling me from head to toe.

"What would you like to dine on this evening, sir?" The waiter asked.

He was a huge mountain of a man, but that'd never stopped me from opening my mouth before. And I'd never be able to look away from his nametag if I didn't ask. Reaching a hand out, I said, "I'm Jesse. Nice to meet you . . . ?"

"Balasz."

Ending with a soft J and emphasis on the second syllable, which he drew out, it sounded like Ba-*lahhj*. "What nationality?" I asked, trying to see around his arm at the rest of his nametag.

"Hungarian." He pressed tight a thin smile. "For you for dinner?"

"Oh, um." I glanced back at the menu. "I'll have the soup for starters. How're the scallops compared to the prime rib?"

He scribbled. "Soup, scallops, prime rib."

"Oh, no, not both. Which would you recommend?"

"Both." He took a step toward my dad.

"Balasz, I can't eat all that."

"No problem, Jesse. You eat what you can. Enjoy. Feast."

"No soup then, okay?"

"Oh, but soup is good. You'll see."

"Balasz."

He put his hand up. "Trust me."

Slumping back in my seat, I turned to Navy, who was smirking—but *with* me, I was pretty sure this time, not at me. I sighed into it, needing some sort of distraction.

I'd been leaving messages for my mom the whole drive out to Seattle, and ten minutes ago she finally texted me back.

A text.

I'll leave some soup in the fridge for when you get home,

okay? This was a far cry from answering any of the questions I'd left on her voicemail.

My head shot back to my dad. "You did not just order a bourbon for dinner," I hissed, as Balasz moved on to Isaiah.

"Nope. I ordered three."

Isaiah

I'd thought about sitting next to her. But then I'd have been the creepy new guy. What were the odds there'd be another person our age at the table? He was twitchy at least. No way she'd go for that, classy show mare that she was. She might be trying to hide it with the white tee and jeans, but the way she held herself? There was no doubt.

Plus, he downed his entire meal like he was eating out of a trough.

Jesse pushed back in his seat. "I'm gonna head up to the teen lounge. You guys wanna come?"

I snorted, and Navy stared at him. Yeah, and he still felt the need to be babysat. I had this in the bag.

"All right, well, maybe I'll catch you later." Jesse glanced at his dad. Dude was staring into his third drink. "See you back at the room?"

Navy's mom—*It's Delilah, but you can call me Dee*—said, "Navy will go with you, dear. She was saying on the way in how enjoyable it sounded."

Navy rolled her head dramatically to stare at her mother.

Delilah patted Navy's hand with a smile, then leaned in to whisper in her ear. Navy stood, tossing her napkin on the table.

I got up too. "If this is as lame as I think it's gonna be, we're out of there in fifteen minutes."

"Zay—"

"Yeah, Gram, I know." I cut her off before she could announce that I had a curfew. She wanted me back before she fell asleep. Said she spent enough time worrying about me when I was gone at the ranch.

Worry, worry, worry. She thought she could worry me happy. It made sense five years ago, but things were better now.

Nodding, she slipped her hand in mine and squeezed, holding tight until I did the same. Which I did, to reassure her for all the times she'd used that squeeze to reassure me.

As soon as we were away from the table, Jesse started nickering. "Isn't this cool? I didn't actually think it would look like the Titanic, but it's like we're stuck in the movie. This is the crazy biggest ship I've ever been on, let alone seen. You guys ever been on a cruise before? I keep getting lost. It's like you need a compass in here . . ."

He was right. We didn't know how to get around. Took us ten times longer than it should have to find the elevator. Or felt like it because of his constant stream of consciousness.

When we finally swung into the right alcove, preppy boy from the line was there. Done up in an outfit that wouldn't last through a day of real work. He spotted Jesse first, since he was making all the noise. When he saw me, a smile busted out of his lips.

"Hey, Cowboy." He ran a hand through his hair. "You guys heading up to the teen lounge?"

"That we are," Jesse replied, reaching a hand out.

"Bern. Nice to meet you."

"Jesse." Nodding to drive this home, he motioned to Navy. "This is Navy, and the cowboy is Isaiah."

Bern rocked back on his dress shoes. "Isaiah's nice, but I prefer Cowboy."

Great. Just what I needed. And no way could I be a dick about it. I didn't have it in me.

I sidled closer to Navy, a hint for him if he were willing to notice it. She took a step away, like she could've sensed I was behind her even if she had blinders on. Maybe Aunt Ethel's first impression was right. Maybe she was mean and prissy.

"Do you know where we're going, Bern?" Navy asked, as the door dinged open.

"I sure do." He stepped onto the elevator. "Deck seventeen." Then he side-eyed Jesse's tattooed bicep. "You play piano or something?"

"No. I mean, someday hopefully. I'm just really into music. Instrumental, actually. And this was cooler than a violin. Violins might be my favorite. I love when it's just one instrument too, there's this lonely quality about it, you know?

Like it's reaching out to speak to you—"

"You're an odd dude," Bern interrupted. "I think we're gonna get along just fine."

But he was looking at me when he said it.

ACKNOWLEDGMENTS

This book was a hard one with many stops and starts. It was the first time I changed a climax and pulled a plotline. Thus, I'm especially thankful to those who helped me with the crafting of the book: Kat Abbott for reading this twice and forcing my hand on adding a scene to the beginning. Mairead Ahmed for relentlessly asking if that needs to be a question (and part of the relentlessness is just in my head, hearing your voice as I write now). Eden is maybe the hardest character I've had to write, and I like to think your aversion to internal questions helped her be a little less whiny, a little more convicted. Karla Manternach for peering into it, identifying all my themes and intentions, and telling me where they fell flat. This book leveled itself up because of you. Thank you also to other early readers: Jeff Schill, Nancy McConnell, and those in the distant past.

Related to the production: Thank you Robin Vuchnich for the amazing cover, once again. They just keep getting better! Staci Frenes for your copy edits, and Michelle Mercier and Lauren Marcu for final eyes. Thank you to Emma Peters for beta reading, and for being the kind of person I can trust to look at a book the same way I do. You reading is like me reading with fresh eyes—truly valuable and not something many authors have in their back pocket. Finally, a nod to National Geographic, who brought me the article on plastic that Billie quotes at the bar.

Putting a clean novel out in the world truly takes a village. And by village I mean many, many eyes and double checks (perhaps there will never be enough), so, ultimately, thank you to those who lent fresh eyes—thank you to my village.